VEGANZA

ANIMAL HEROES SERIES

LIBERATION

**Animal Hero Kids –
Voices for the Voiceless**
(Vol. 1, 2014 and Vol. 2, 2019)

Veganza Animal Hero
a picture book (2020)

The Heart Whisperer

One woman's' pursuit to push the boundaries of our compassion

April 23, 2022

A new short documentary by Shaun Monson, the creator of the groundbreaking film, *Earthlings*, with a cameo by Joaquin Phoenix, features never before seen footage of wildlife releases and activism in action.

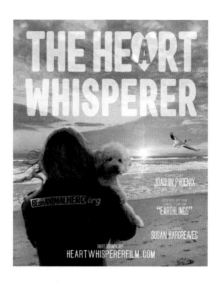

Veganza Animal Hero Claymation

April 23, 2022

Help continue Susan's work empowering others to be animal heroes to all species.

"I thank you, Susan, for all that you do in your community, for daring to innovate, for dreaming big, and for finding ways to create a better, kinder tomorrow." —**Michelle Obama**

"Susan Hargreaves' latest creation continues her decades-long work to engage the imagination and the heart to consider all species are interconnected. She understands our endless potential for adventure, magic and sanctuary as we are whisked away into the wonderful world of Veganza Animal Heroes. —**Ingrid Newkirk, founder of the largest animal rights group in the world, PETA**

"I was an animal hero at 3 years old when I felt that animals had the right to live free of harm and suffering. Susan's vital work to foster empathy and critical thinking leads to compassionate action, and ultimately, a more peaceful world for all." —**Joaquin Phoenix**

"Susan Hargreaves' skill and ingenuity as a humane educator are vitally needed… It is precisely the type of outstanding educational programs and resources Susan creates that greatly benefits any community."
—**Jane Goodall**

"How beautiful to equate the word "hero" with empathy and compassion for animals, qualities that children so naturally possess."
—**Maggie Baird, Billie Eilish's mother**

"Animal Heroes Rock! The good news is we can all help animals in need."
—**Sir Paul McCartney**

"The world being a kinder place is what we're all about. Susan Hargreaves inspires all ages to be animal heroes. Veganza Animal Heroes is uplifting, empowering and exactly what the world needs right now."
—**Dave & Steve Flynn, The Happy Pear**

VEGANZA

ANIMAL HEROES SERIES

LIBERATION

SUSAN HARGREAVES

Illustrated by Monique Martinez

Be an Animal Hero Press
A division of animalherokids.org

Publisher: Be an Animal Hero Press, A division of animalherokids.org

ISBN (paperback): 978-1-7357399-5-3
ISBN (hardcover): 978-1-7357399-4-6
ISBN (ebook): 978-1-7357399-3-9

Illustrated by Monique Martinez
Edited by Tanjah Karvonen
Layout and design by Kim Monteforte

Printed by Amazon KDP, USA

Please contact Animal Hero Kids for permissions:

Susan Hargreaves, Founder
Animal Hero Kids
10152 Indiantown Road, Suite 146
Jupiter, FL 33478 USA
susanh@animalherokids.org
animalherokids.org

I dedicate this book to all of the phoenixes who
rise from the ashes, to those who persist in striving
to make a dent in the hard shell of cruel apathy and
to those individuals who are open to discovering
how to transform and save the lives of others by
assessing the impact of their daily choices. This
tale of a magical world of daring rescues, incredible
earthlings, epiphanies and "veganiphanies" is
written for each and every one of you.

—*Susan Hargreaves*

TABLE OF CONTENTS

VEGANZA ANIMAL HEROES – LIBERATION CHARACTER LIST

Note: If you wish to perform this novel/story as a play, here is the list of characters it features. To aid with play productions, each scene is delineated with titles to signify scene changes.

Characters in Alphabetical Order

Anderson Cooper – reporter extraordinaire

Angela Means – vegan soul food entrepreneur

Anita Kranjc – Animal Save Movement founder

Billie – a surprise visitor

Bubba – Florida Governor

Connor – Irish wolfhound mix rescued dog

Courage – the vegan mermaid who defends all the sea creatures

Danu – Irish matriarch, Veganza's mother

Darragh Flynn – a Happy Pear brother who may not be as well-known as his brothers yet, but just as warm-hearted and genuine

Freedom – the superhero who can marshal the air and all of the species who fly in a powerful force for animal liberation

Happy Pear Twins – Dave & Steve Flynn, vegan brothers at the helm of an Irish vegan mecca

Heart – Michael Daniel, the truck driver's vegan daughter

Irene – foster group home counselor

Jules – the crow messenger and global news reporter

Khendall – a young Animal Hero Crew activist

Lolita – the orca who has been captive since 1970 floating endlessly and alone in her watery prison

Lovey – 22-year-old canine rescued by Veganza, she was found wandering in the Everglades, and now enjoys her adventures and "furever" home

Maggie – Billie's mother and vegan food advocate, founder of Support and Feed

Michael Daniel – a transport truck driver with a developing conscience

Midnight – a feline stray needing rescue

Pharrell – a surprise guest

Phoenix – a teen hero who does not know how strong and resilient she is

Rick – a Native American teen resident at the foster group home

Ron Nistico Palamara – a kind counselor from the foster group home

Sara – The Happy Pear media-savvy maven

Security Guard (Chuck) – Miami Seaquarium security guard

Tara – Khendall's mother and animal activist

Vanetta – a teen resident at the foster group home

Veganza – the ginger-haired superhero who lives in a Florida banyan tree who uses her powers of freezing scenes and speaking to the conscience to instill empathy

CHAPTER 1

Veganza

The sounds of the Everglades waking up emanated through the top canopy of the mangrove leaves as a sleek black crow flew through the blooming, steamy morning mist. His wings flapped through the middle of the mangroves and he swooped down swiftly to land on an outstretched banyan tree branch. "Caww Caww!"

A hanging clump of Spanish moss was flicked to the side as a bright blue eye peered out from a small hole in the root covered tree trunk. "Jules, good morning, I was just about to pour my morning tea and enjoy a bit of ginger spice cake. Join me." The crow ducked his head through the tree trunk's opening and the rest of the face and figure belonging to the eye came into full view.

A fine strong clear face it was, with wide set eyes and a resolute chin. She turned towards a sea grape leaf covered table. Her long waves of strawberry blonde hair rippled down her back as she walked across the interior cocoon of her banyan tree home. A network of woody roots and branches interconnected to create sturdy walls. At the base of one of the walls slept an ancient, small poodle type dog named Lovey. She lifted her head up to gaze steadily at Jules the crow as he landed. Normally, a companion canine would have had no place in this forest setting. However, Lovey had been abandoned off US Highway 27 near where the Florida Everglades begin. Veganza felt she had to offer the petrified dog a "furever" home filled with love. Her haven felt more like a home with the addition of Lovey's calm presence and undemanding company.

Veganza, the superhero animal defender, had left her Irish native land to explore the world and decided she quite liked the warmth of the Florida sun and the feel of the moist air on her skin. She had fond memories of her earlier life nestled in the emerald green Wicklow Mountains and her unique family. Veganza's blue hued transparent wings had carried her across the waves, her magnificent green velvet cape billowing behind her. She held tight to her gift from her grandparents: a magic, ivy-covered Irish black-thorn branch. The hooked cane stops danger by freezing scenes when needed only when Veganza wields it. When Veganza uses her magical powers, the perpetrators feel exactly what their victims feel. This realization of another's suffering causes an increased sense of empathy. Veganza, unlike her fellow animal superhero defenders, often relies on a network of determined, kind humans for assistance. The humans she chooses will go above and beyond to save another being from suffering.

Veganza sat in her chair formed out of a mix of roots, wild orchids and moss. She poured fragrant hibiscus tea from her glass teapot into a translucent crystal cup. She poured water into a stone bowl on the table for Jules. A

similar crystal bowl sparkled with spring water.The moist ginger spice cake was the perfect accompaniment for tea.

"What's the morning news?" asked Veganza as Jules the crow pointed his closed umbrella shaped beak upwards as the liquid of cool hibiscus tea travelled down his throat.

"Human animals appointed by the Florida Governor at the Florida Fish and Wildlife Commission want to make money by selling hunting permits to kill black bear families. A mass group of hunters invading our homes with intent to kill starts this Saturday," squawked Jules. "This gives us very little time to stop the massacre," Veganza said as she turned and waved her palm over the tree trunk's interior wall. A screen appeared. A red shouldered hawk on the Animal Voices News Service was saying, "This is a red alert! All bears must stock up on food and water. Humans will be using false calls and food lures. Ignore them. Keep your cubs with you at all times. Every family needs to stay hidden for two complete days. Animal Voices News Service will keep you posted to let you know when it's safe to leave your hiding places. Our flying hawk eyewitness reported that a human news conference will be broadcast on the human news today from Tallahassee at the Florida State capital building." Veganza waved the screen to darkness.

"We have no time to waste. This could be a full bear family massacre." Veganza swiftly placed her long green mossy cloak over her shoulders which hung on a nearby bougainvillea wall hook. Lovey jumped into Veganza's arms, her head leaned into Veganza's shoulder, "This is one mission I know I can help with."

"Veganza to the rescue!" said Veganza as she raised her fist upwards in the universal salute of justice. The leaf dappled roof opened to reveal a Florida technicolor blue sky as Veganza's wings powerfully arched upwards, swiftly lifting her and Lovey directly up and out of her banyan tree home.

CHAPTER 2

Intervention

eganza surveyed the scene below as her flying figure, blue wings outstretched, approached the giant
dome of the Tallahassee state capital building. She
heard the chants and saw the assembled protestors from
her aerial view, "Stop the Kill, Stop the Kill!" Veganza and
Lovey landed to perch on the side of the dome. She had
no fear of discovery. If anyone looked up, once she put her
cloak on, no human animal could see her or anyone she
holds in her arms.

She read the demonstrators' signs with her hawk eye
vision, another one of her many superpowers: "Bears are
not trophies!" "Real men are kind," proclaimed the state-
ments on the signs. She could also see reporters with live
broadcast news trucks interviewing the protestors below.
There was a police yellow "Do not cross" divider tape to

separate the group of big-bellied hunters dressed in camouflage, who were yelling from the sidelines. Some were armed with rifles strapped to their backs.

Veganza landed on the side of the dome. "Humans! It's a wonder we can find any young animal heroes to train when they sprout from this convoluted mess of conflicted humanity. I have said it before and I will say it again, Lovey, it always comes down to one of two things, money or ego getting in the way of integrity and kindness." Lovey answered with one of her signature growls which can mean many different things. It could be interpreted as a sound for both agreement and literal disgruntlement.

A cheer suddenly erupted from the crowd. Television cameras turned to film the unfurling of a two-story long banner being dropped from the bridge across the road. The two-story long banner had a close-up artist's image of a bear's face and the words: "NO KILLING!" and BEanANIMALHERO.org emblazoned on it. Another similar banner was hanging from the building.

"Right, time for action," said Veganza to Lovey. "Hold on!" and they flew seamlessly through a closed window on the top floor of the capital building.

Subterfuge

"How many out of state permits have we sold so far at 300 bucks a pop?" asked Florida Governor Beauregard Bubba. "So far we have made $376,900 from selling 3,778 in and out of state, hunting permits," said Florida Fish and Wildlife (FWC) Governor appointed Commissioner Slaughter. "How the deuce are we gettin away with making the Florida public believe we will only harvest 320 bears?" asked the Governor. "So far only the animal activists are investigating enough to do the true math. We are saying we will stop the hunt when 320 bears are killed and no one but the activists

are asking how we are going to let the almost 3,800 hunters hunting in the forests of the taxpayer paid-for "refuges" know when to stop killing bears. This is going to be a glorious bloody day," said the Commissioner.

"I hope we don't hear those tree-hugging animal lovers during our news conference. Our room is soundproof," said the Governor. "It don't matter anyhow. Thanks to you and the 'state of the art' bear counting. As long as you put those words 'state of the art' before anything we say, it's in the bag." The Commissioner clapped Beauregard on the back. "I'll see you down there, Bubba boy. We're loaded for bear," said the Commissioner, as he pointed an imaginary rifle at the door, "Bang, Bang!"

The Governor typed his name into the Google search bar on his cell phone to see if any news items had appeared where his name had been mentioned. Nope, no new articles yet. An odd scratching sound was coming from the other side of his office door. The noise interrupted the Governor as he started to put on his navy-blue suit jacket and straighten his red tie. He presses the intercom on his desk, "Doris I don't care who that is. It's your job to send them away. Get rid of them." And still the scratching continued. He walks over and opens it, and sees no one as he looks straight ahead, then looks down.

"What the dang! What are you doing here? Are you lost, little fella?" Bubba hunkers down to pet Lovey behind the ears. "You look just like my little Benji Dog, first name Benji, last name Dog. I had him when I was just a pup." Lovey stands up on her back legs and licks the pinkish nose of the Governor and looks intently into his eyes. They face each other. Bubba sees the wisdom, life and personality shining through Lovey's eyes. Their eyes lock. Bubba freezes as Veganza's cane leads the way through the wall behind him. "Good job opening his heart, Lovey. Back to a time he had long forgotten. Now, I will do the rest."

Veganza strides over to lock the door before placing her open hand, gently, on the Governor's forehead. His entire body is like a frozen ice sculpture. He's in a dreamlike sleep state, with his eyes wide open and his expression utterly still. "You are a mother bear walking in the woods with your two 8-month-old cubs. The joyful way the cubs frolic reminds you of how Benji Dog used to play in your childhood. They jump all over your back as you kneel down to roll and romp. You look into their gleaming, happy eyes and feel their heartbeat next to yours as they fall asleep on your chest, tired, after their wrestle. You are happy. You are content. You are filled with love for your cubs and you enjoy watching the clouds in the sky move above your verdant forest home.

Suddenly, you hear footsteps crunching loudly on the forest floor. Into the clearing appear two men, one with a rifle and one with an automatic cross bow. Each weapon is pointed dead center at your cubs' faces. "Nooo!" You growl as you jump to your feet.

Empathy

Bubba shakes his head and stands up from his position still kneeling on the floor. Veganza is nowhere to be seen. "What the dang heck is going on here." Another noise from the door is heard just as Lovey jumps up into his arms. He opens the door again only to find no one of his height there. He looks down and sees a young teen with a soft afro framing his face wearing a black t-shirt with the words in large white letters "Be an Animal Hero" printed on it. "I was looking for my dog, Mister, thank you for finding her!" "You shouldn't be wandering around here all by your lonesome. Don't you have a mother looking for you? What's your name?" asks Bubba. "She was busy talking to the reporters. I had to find Lovey," the boy said as he knelt down to pick up Lovey. "My name's Khendall. I am an animal hero. I speak up for all animals not to be harmed. Will you be an animal hero, too? "Well, I plan to be an animal hero, Khendall, I plan to be."

News Flash

"In an unprecedented announcement today Florida's Governor stated at a Tallahassee capital news conference that he was calling off the family bear massacre," reported Hawkeye on the Animal Voices News Service. Veganza waved her hand in front of the wood grain in her home's tree interior wall. The screen disappeared. Veganza turned to Lovey, "How wonderful. The world has another human animal hero now. All of the bear families in Florida will sleep easier in their dens tonight."

CHAPTER 3

Phoenix

Agirl's head was bowed behind the bathroom door, her hair as glossy as a raven's wing. Her petite frame huddled forward cradling her mobile phone. Her normally animated, brown-eyed gaze was hidden behind closed eyes.

Her stepfather's 200-pound frame was double the size and weight of her mother's. Their dinner lay half eaten, sitting on the plates on the dining room table.

CRASH! The girl heard a loud sound perhaps of a heavy piece of furniture hitting the floor combined with dishes crashing as she crouched in the spot her mother had told her to stay. She was practiced in keeping her cell close by as one never knew what would set off an angry temper tantrum in her mother's husband. She peered closely at the

screen on her cell wondering if this was one of the times she should call the police.

"WHO DO YOU THINK YOU ARE? YOU DON'T EVEN HAVE A COLLEGE DEGREE AND YOU THINK YOU KNOW MORE THAN ME ABOUT AMERICA! WHY DO YOU MAKE ME YELL AT YOU BECAUSE YOU DON'T LISTEN?

She heard her mother's meek, cajoling reply, "I was just saying I think everyone should have health care."

"EVERYTHING YOU HAVE I GAVE YOU!! I AM GOING TO KNOCK SOME SENSE INTO THAT EMPTY LOSER HEAD OF YOURS!"

She called 911 and whispered to the dispatch operator "Please, send help, I think my mother is hurt." She had learned from experience the police arrive much quicker if they think someone is already injured. The operator confirmed the address of the apartment building. "Stay on the line until the police arrive. Are there any weapons in the house? Are you in a safe place with a lock on the door?" "My stepfather is a hunter. He has a shotgun. I am locked in the bathroom. My mother told me to," she whispered.

SMASH! It sounded like dishes were splintering on the hard tile floor.

"The patrol car ETA is 5 more minutes. What's your name and how old are you?"

CLASH!

"Phoenix, thirteen."

"I have to see if my mother is alright."

She dropped the cell phone, unlocked and swung open the door and moved as fast as she could.

Her ears were assailed by the loudness of the television announcer's voice. It was still on the news channel that had started this latest in a long line of unwarranted explosions of anger. A thump, thump heartbeat sound reverberated in her ears as she opened the door. She stepped into a scene she will never forget. Phoenix saw her stepfather push her mothers' one-hundred-pound body by her shoulders into the marble fireplace surround. Phoenix quickly grabbed the closest thing to hand, a tall, heavy crystal vase, she raced forward aiming for the back of his head through his nose as her Dad had taught her to do before the divorce. She swung with every ounce of strength she possessed. He was stunned by the impact at the exact same moment her mother's head hit the solid marble of the fireplace on the way down.

"Police! Open the door!" Phoenix raced past him to unlock the door. Her stepfather tried to hold his nose together as blood spurted through his fingers. A man and woman police officer stepped in quickly. The female officer handcuffed her stepfather's hands behind his back as he wailed, "My nose, my nose." The other officer applied pressure to the back of her mother's head while radioing for an ambulance, as she lay there, motionless. She was more still than Phoenix had ever seen her before.

Journal

Dear reader, let's look over the shoulder of Phoenix, her hair in a braid behind her, as she continues to write her story in her journal.

> … you may wonder why I don't include the name of my mother's husband in the lines of this journal. I vowed never to say or write the name of the man who killed my mother. If that wasn't bad enough, he is also responsible for me ending up here in this grey, linoleum-floored, industrial-green painted foster group home.
>
> My Dad has a new family in Guyana now and his new young wife doesn't want any reminders of his first family life. So here, alone I sit, wondering, as I write, will my life ever get better?

CHAPTER 4

Defenders

"Ha, ha. You can't reach, shorty," said Vanetta, holding a crying black kitten high above her head as Phoenix tried to jump up to save the kitten while she meowed loudly. Phoenix knew she should not have come on this foster home group trip to the ocean. There were not enough adults to watch everyone and it was harder to see in the darkening sky. "Here, catch!" Vanetta called to Rick, who was standing about seven feet away. The cat's meow and Phoenix's pleas blended loudly into one big Meowwwnooooooo... A band of moving smokey light undulated towards the scene as rays of light encircled the group.

Suddenly, Vanetta froze, and so did Rick and the little black kitten, too. Phoenix was stunned to stillness, as an apparition appeared before her. A ginger-haired creature with blue wings and a forest-green velvet cape landed,

swiftly, at the same time as a tall wave splashed by the shore. The wall of water dropped to reveal a gleaming mermaid using the curve at the base of her tail to stand tall.

Vanetta and Rick, even though they were frozen, began to feel the same degree of fear that the kitten had felt. Veganza looked at Phoenix, and spoke to Courage, "This one is not frozen. Can you see us?" "Who... who... wha... what, are you, two?" stuttered the shocked Phoenix.

"Looks like we may have found another sincere, kind, empathetic human to help. It has to be the only reason she's not frozen, too," said Courage to Veganza.

"To answer your question, I'm Veganza." "I'm Courage," said the mermaid. "We are part of the Veganza Animal Hero Crew. We unite to defend the defenseless," said Veganza and Courage together, their voices echoing in harmony.

Phoenix was speechless and trepidatious, as she stared at these two unbelievable looking magical beings before her. Veganza, her strawberry blonde hair shining in the moonlight, stood in a capable pose looking down at Phoenix. The fascinating, luminescent scales of Courage's tail twinkled in the moonlight as the mermaid looked intently into Phoenix's shocked face.

Veganza walked close to the side of Vanetta's face and whispered softly in her ear, "You will be a voice for the voiceless. Your words and music in song will open closed hearts." She repeated the exact same thing in Rick's ear.

"You may have suffered to understand so keenly what suffering is. You may not appreciate it yet, but your increased sense of empathy is your superpower," said Veganza to Phoenix. "We need a human such as you. Will you help us with our next mission?" asked Courage in her deep voice. Phoenix replied, "I don't know. Things don't really turn out that well for me. I am not strong, really, and I am pretty short, and my hands are kind of full right now with trying to cope with living in this new foster group home."

"Have you ever felt trapped? Have you ever felt hopeless and helpless?" asked Veganza. "Would you like to ensure a certain orca who has spent over 50 years in a prison is free?" queried Courage.

Despite her misgivings, Phoenix began to slowly nod a yes. "We'll be in touch," promised Veganza. She flew in an upwards trajectory and disappeared into the night sky. Courage splashed a speedy, spiral turn of her tail and vanished under the waves.

"What am I doing?" asked Vanetta as she and Rick and the little black kitten all came out of their frozen state. "I am so sorry, little kitty." "Oh, we need to make sure this little guy is not hungry and has a safe home," said Vanetta. "Let's ask Irene, our foster mom, if we can adopt him or her," said Rick. "We are sorry Phoenix. Our bad. We know now that we have to help animals in trouble. They're just like us, really."

"I know. I have a great idea. Let's start a band and educate people through our music," said Vanetta. "I can't believe it. I was just going to say that exact same thing! What a coincidence!" replied Rick.

Maybe things won't stay completely bad after all, thought Phoenix.

CHAPTER 5

Freedom

Veganza and Courage sang out in harmony, their strong, clear voices echoing like a gospel choir across the sky, "Freedom, Freedom, Freedom!" Veganza stood on the rocky shoreline in Hobe Sound, Florida. The place was known locally as Blowing Rock. It was named for the spouts of water spurting upwards through the holes in the rock base every time a wave crashes in. It was a secluded place with pelicans diving and small killdeer darting back and forth with the tide. The sunrise cast a pinkish purple glow on the scene.

Courage and Veganza's heads were side by side, at an even height as they sang out. Courage sat; her magnificent, gleaming, green gold tail lay beside her on the glossy rock. Veganza stood with her green, velvety cape flowing in the morning breeze, her luminescent blue wings fanned out behind her. One head with hair so dark it gleamed almost a deep purple color, her coppery skin glowed, and the other head with fire-gold hair and the moon-colored skin of Ireland. The two longtime friends, both warriors for animals, continued to ring out together in harmony "Freedom!"

A cloud floated forward as it came closer to the two animal defenders. An incredible looking being came into sight. He was sitting cross-legged on top of the approaching cloud. Behind him floated a waist-length cloud patterned cape. His defined chest muscles displayed the same letter V for the word vegan, that was emblazoned on Veganza's body suit.

His perfectly shaped oval head turned to the pair. His kind brown eyes lit up his warm bronze face with a big smile. "Hey, good to see my two favorite sistahs. What's up?" Freedom's superpowers can marshal the force of the sky, winds, storms and all of the flying creatures to unite together in a strong common cause of animal rescue.

"It's past time to liberate the trapped orca from the cement tank in Miami. She needs to get back to her home in the waters off the San Juan Islands. The Lummi Nations people have her sea-side pen ready for her gradual release and return to her family pod," said Courage. "We cannot afford to wait. Lolita's heart is breaking. Her morale is the lowest it has ever been. She's been utterly alone for decades. We now know of a human teen who can be completely trusted to help," Veganza said. "I have an idea or two which I think will work," replied Freedom.

The Veganza Animal Hero Crew gathered closer together, enjoying the stuffed pasta shells provided by Courage. A bystander would have heard the use of some of the heroes' favorite words, words they loved to speak, words like freedom, rescue and liberation.

Liberation

There is no real sea with miles to swim in at the Miami Seaquarium. This is the main problem for all of the sea creatures imprisoned there. It's a cement grave for the living. The captors profit off their captives' misery. Slowly, the public is catching on, yet, not fast enough for the creatures still held within its concrete walls. Lolita the orca barely swam, her 21-foot body, circling slowly, again and again, in her 35-foot-wide tank, around, and around, and around. She has repeated these same movements in this same space in the same dismal circle ever since her capture in 1970 at only 4 years of age from Penn Cove, in Puget Sound.

The full moon reflects on the inky waters of Biscayne Bay rippling, reflecting, so tantalizingly close to Lolita's watery jail cell.

The sounds of an electric guitar and three amplified voices singing in harmony travel across the empty metal seats over to Lolita's tank.

Free in the sea,
is how they're meant to be,
who are we to jail them?
they need to go back to their family
yes, Free in the Sea,
is the only way to be.

The song's melodic refrain was accompanied by Vanetta on the drums. A black van's headlights illuminated the scene. A camera on a tripod was recording the group. Rick strummed his guitar and Phoenix sang at her stand-up microphone. Vanetta's drums had the word LIBERTY emblazoned on the big bass drum. A lone security guard drove his patrol car out to the aquarium's entrance where, Phoenix, Vanetta and Rick had set up their new band's sound equipment. Thanks to a music grant, Ron, their counselor, had helped them apply for, their band called LIBERTY was now fully outfitted to practice. All of the equipment and the three teens all fit in Ron's van, including a generator to power the amplifiers.

"You can't play that music here," said the security guard. Ron extended his hand to the guard in an attempt to diffuse the situation. "Ciao. I'm Ron Nistico Palamara. What's your name?" "Chuck, and you still can't play that music here." "I am aware that we are on public property. We are on a public thoroughfare. Local bylaws allow for this band to play here as long as it is not after eleven."

"We are filming a video for our new song," piped in Phoenix. "This is the perfect setting." Vanetta raised her drumstick to get Phoenix and Rick's attention. "Take it from the top." The chords of the electric guitar were joined by the loud clash of the symbols attached to the drum set.

"Perhaps you would be so kind as to talk with me over here, sir. I am sure we can come up with a solution that's good for us all," said Ron. He was just about to lead the security guard a little further away from the entrance to talk when a black car with tinted windows arrived in the parking lot beside them. A singing phenomenon named Billie and her mother stepped out. "Billie, Maggie!" said Phoenix, Vanetta and Rick in unison. The security guard stopped and stared. "Yeah, I saw your Insta-post. Break a leg with your new band," said the young woman wearing techno-green baggy pants. Maggie, the always supportive mother, with soft auburn hair, wore a t-shirt with the words Support + Feed emblazoned on it in the same technicolor as her daughter's pants. She extended her hand to Phoenix. "Here are tickets to tomorrow night's Miami arena show and gift certificates to a vegan restaurant for dinner for the entire group home," said Billie's mother.

"Excuse me, can you please sign this for my daughter?" asked Chuck, the security guard. "Sure. Now we have to

fly," said Billie, and off Maggie and Billie went. The three teens couldn't believe it and took it as a sign that there were more good things ahead.

Chuck knew his daughter was going to be thrilled as he put his notepad with Billie's signature in his pocket. He turned to Ron and they walked with their backs turned from the now louder music away from the Miami Seaquarium to talk.

Freedom was cloaked in his night sky cape, invisible to all human eyes. Veganza's peacock blue wings soundlessly powered her through the sky. Both heroes were surrounded by flocks of pelicans, holding in their beaks a heavy-duty piece of rubber sheeting. What a spectacle the night sky displayed as Veganza and at least 50 pelicans all dived towards Lolita's cement tank. Lolita looked up, alone in her tank for so very long. She raised her head and dared to think, "Could this be it? Could this be my rescue at last?"

In one unified swoop, the pelicans dove under Lolita, securing the sturdy rubber sheeting in place. Freedom marshalled the strength of the air. "1, 2, 3, all together now," whispered Veganza, and with one big swoosh! Lolita was lifted out of her prison for the first time in 52 years. Freedom's muscular arms strained as they were raised with his hands placed under the hammock-shaped conveyance. The power of the wind assisted their purpose and propelled forward the 7,000-pound orca with Freedom and the pelicans' flight power.

"You're going home. No need to worry," murmured Veganza as she flew beside Lolita, keeping her calm. Her hand was placed gently on Lolita to monitor the orca's steady heartbeat.

CHAPTER 6

Return

A nd the band played on…

We are LIBERTY, the band,
Our message sings out across the land,
Join our voices in song,
Freedom is coming, it won't be long.

"It's five minutes to eleven and I will be calling the police under the local noise ordinance, and you will all be ticketed," yelled the now fully exasperated security guard. He held his cell phone with one hand ready to call. "I understand that you have a job to do," Ron replied patiently, "yet, these teens are excited for the first time in months. The global non-profit *Be an Animal Hero* will be releasing this video on all their social media channels. I rented this night vision camera at considerable expense. Why not just give them this opportunity? They have had such a rough time of it, so far, in their short lives. We are in fact on a public sidewalk, not on Miami Seaquarium property."

"Alright, alright. I've got teenagers at home. I do have a heart. Between you and me, ticket sales are so low right now. I am looking for another job, anyway. There's no job security in this keeping wildlife captive business anymore," replied the security guard. Ron leaned in, "I think I can help you with a potential new job..."

Home

"Welcome back to the sea, my friend!" Courage's luminescent sea green scaled tail glistened in the moonlight. Her shiny black hair streamed behind her. Lolita landed softly beside her in the sea as the pelicans flew away with the rubber sheeting to hide any evidence of the nighttime liberation. "Follow me around this turn. We have a long journey ahead. My sea friends are here to help you rest whenever you feel the need to along the way. You can swim or be kept afloat until we get you back to your home waters."

Veganza and Freedom waved from the sky as Courage led the orca on her return journey. More and more dolphins, sharks and sea turtles joined the liberation trip, each ready to help bear her weight for periodic rests. The swimmers had six and a half hours until sunrise. Everyone raced against time. The combined surge resulted in an increase in speed thanks to the sea travelers carrying the orca's weight on their backs, on their shoulders and on their shells. Lolita had been in her lonely tank for so long that their help and company were like a dream. The Florida sea creatures flowed forward to the San Juan Islands as Courage led the way.

Liberty

Veganza and Freedom return to the scene of the liberation. They swooped down to whisper encouragements to the still captive dolphins. "We will be back another night next week for your rescue, too," intones Freedom's deep voice. "Don't lose hope," whispers Veganza.

Overhead and out of the sightline of the security guard Veganza and Freedom flew. Freedom's night cape ensured that he still could not be seen. Veganza gave a thumbs up to the three big-hearted teens who proceeded to proudly sing louder, looking at each other with triumphant glee in their eyes. Unaware of the flying heroes above, the security guard and Ron carried on their conversation about jobs with a future in an ethically evolving world.

Sunrise

The peach-colored rays of the sunrise reflected on the waves near Penn Cove. More ocean species joined the victorious return of the formerly lonely orca to her home waters. Lolita opened her eyes as she passed Penn Cove, the scene of her capture using speedboats, an airplane and explosives. Five orcas died that day on August 8th in 1970. She was able to sleep, and yet, still travel at top speed thanks to the assistance of a growing number of sea creatures floating her forward. An assortment of fins, tails, scales and shells could be seen populating the sea's surface in a flurry of movement. The last survivor of the forty orcas captured in Penn Cove swam closer to her destination.

A fast and urgent high frequency squeaky whistling cried under the waves, "Is that you? Is that you?" The sound echoed in the unique language belonging to the Southern Resident Orca L pod. Ocean Sun, L25, named and identified by the local non-profit group, Orca Network, is now 90 years of age and is Lolita's mother.

Ocean Sun torpedoed forward. "My baby, my baby, you're back! I never thought this day would come." The two orcas floated heart to heart, in a state of euphoric joy.

Being once again with her mother and her home pod was comforting enough to wash away the years of abject loneliness, misery and despair. The orca who would no longer be known by her human captors' given name breathed a deep, sighing sound of relief. The sound needed no translation. It was universal. It was timeless. Every sea creature, including Courage, was still and yet, moved, upon hearing it.

A gradual release sea pen had been created by the local Lummi Nation. In their language, they refer to the orcas as "lhol mechen," which means "our relations under the waves." The orca's mother explained to her once lost daughter how her family pod would be staying right beside the sea pen until she was used to diving deeply again.

Breaking News

Phoenix, Vanetta, Rick and the other teen residents and their counselor, Ron, sat around the picnic table in the yard at the foster group home, basking in the early morning Florida sunshine. A large cast iron frying pan of scramble fried tofu and vegan sausages sent a tantalizing aroma up from the center of the picnic table. Toast, bagels and a selection of *Miyoko's*, *Kite Hill*, *Follow Your Heart* and *Daiya* vegan cheeses and tomato slices accompanied their weekend breakfast. Rick snapped a photo of the breakfast spread with his phone to post later.

Since Phoenix, Vanetta, and Rick had become vegan, joining Ron who had been vegan since way back in 1981, everyone agreed it would be easier to serve vegan meals instead of cooking and buying for different meals for everyone. Midnight, the black cat, whose cries were answered by Veganza and Courage, rumbled with purrs as she sat looking out of the window at her kind adopted family.

The smooth tones of the WLRN National Public Radio announcer could be heard through the open kitchen

window. "A mystery has baffled Miami officials and the Mexican conglomerate, the Dolphin Company, owners of the Miami Seaquarium today when an extremely controversial orca tank was discovered to be empty. Is it a coincidence that Lolita was captured on this day, August 8th, 52 years ago? What happened? How can a 21-foot orca weighing 7,000 pounds simply disappear overnight? A summer tropical rainstorm has washed away any possible evidence to be found, reported local police. Stay tuned for updates to your local NPR station."

The teen friends and Ron raised their eyebrows and exchanged looks. Their hands met and clapped in the center of the table as a congratulatory "ALRIGHT!!" could be heard around the Miami neighborhood.

True Freedom

Fast forward now. The Lummi Nation and the animal activists who could afford the trip, and who had spent much of their lives educating and organizing for wildlife to stay in their homes in the wild, all gathered quietly on the shore by the sea pen. A nearby reporter spoke to the live eye camera, "We will soon witness the heartwarming reunion of a family here in Puget Sound. Behind me you can see the three joined populations of the Southern Resident Orca pod, referred to as pods J, K and L. We have witnessed their pods joining at times of birth and now today they have joined at this time of freedom and reunion. Two weeks have passed since the Lummi Nation elder discovered that the orca who was captured 52 years ago had miraculously landed in the sea pen. No one could explain it.

The Miami Seaquarium owners and the Mexican captive marine mammal company acquiesced amid a huge outpouring of public support thanks to the success of a hit song "Free in the Sea" by the new Miami teen band

LIBERTY. We may never know the full story behind the events leading up to today's momentous occasion, but what we do know, is there sure is a lot of orca excitement behind me right now. Their jubilance is equally matched by the human crowd. Look at all that breaching and leaping into the air right beside the sea pen. I see the Lummi Nation elder and a young girl in a boat now opening the sea pen. Look at that orca go! Looks like they all dived under the waves at the same time! I have never seen anything like this in all of my years of reporting the news in our fine state of Washington."

The crowd collectively held its breath, some with their arms extended to hold their cell phone cameras up, as they all watched, riveted, to the spot in the sea where the orca pod had just dived. Even the younger children were still staring at the now disappearing waves. The entire joint orca population had disappeared under the waves all together.

Then up jumped the formerly captive orca, recognizable by her drooped dorsal fin. She spouts water as all of the other area orca pods follow. Each extended orca family member surrounds mother and daughter as they, literally, as they say, hightail it out of there, into the widest open area of the sea.

Tears ran down the face of the reporter. Children jumped up and down with joy. The crowd clapped, their jubilant cheers rang out across the waves as the orcas turned and swam out of sight. Finally, a family was reunited and free.

CHAPTER 7

Strategy

The bright blue sky illuminated a mossy covered table. It looked like it had always been there, near the opening of the forest. The table was an organic, growing piece of art, as natural as the large, smooth grey stones which surrounded it by the shores of the ocean.

A giant wave crashed high on the rock beside the table and the disappearing crest of the surf revealed a gleaming, green-scaled mermaid, her luxuriant hair as dark and shiny as a wet seal. She placed her miraculous tail around the smooth rock base and raised her profile to feel the sun on her face.

In the sky was a spectacularly ethereal figure approaching. Her long green hooded velvet cape and shimmering azure wings could be seen flying in at high velocity. Lovey, her curly haired canine companion, nestled her head, securely, under Veganza's chin.

Veganza and Lovey landed swiftly by the mossy green table and greet their true friend and fellow defender, Courage, with the universal V sign. In the animal hero world they inhabit, V symbolizes the word Vegan and also doubles as the traditional sign denoting Victory.

"Freedom, Freedom, Freedom!" the two strong superheroes chanted across the sea, their melodic voices melding together towards the sky.

The clouds above their head parted to reveal Freedom lounging on the clouds' surface, his chiseled chin resting on one of his hands. The other arm was outstretched as his hand made the same V for Vegan and Victory sign as he faced his animal liberation compatriots.

Courage waved her hand in the direction of the table and a feast of crabless cakes appeared, accompanied by creamy vegan mayonnaise with fresh sprigs of dill, in a stone bowl, for all to enjoy. Courage knew this was Lovey's favorite dish. They all gathered closer to enjoy the scrumptious vegan feast.

"The ripple effects of our most recent liberation tale have now achieved the banning of captive wildlife across the globe," reported Courage. "Now we need a similar plan to trigger the human animals' evolution away from the exploiting and harming or killing of other animals," spoke Freedom, between savoring bites of the moist crabless cakes.

"Phoenix and her friends have proven to be determined yet discreet. Their musical message has definitely contributed to the recent world ban on keeping wildlife captive. What do you think if... ?" Veganza leaned forward. The heroes' heads met as they conferred and planned together.

Liberty Rang

As long as there's a beat in my heart,
We will always do our part,

Don't mess with them,
We won't mess with you,

We were broken,
Now we are strong,

United, a force to right all the wrong,
Move on over apathy, say bye-bye to hate,
On cruelty and killing, we have closed the gate!

"I think you hit it out of the ballpark with these lyrics, Vanetta," congratulated Phoenix.

"Yeah, we are kicking it! The benefit for the *Be an Animal Hero* empathy empowering, education programs is the perfect place to release this song," said Rick, as he leaned his guitar against the garage wall where the band now practiced after school.

Phoenix finished chewing a big bite of the still warm slice of vegan pizza Ron had brought for the rehearsing band members. He so was proud of his mother's Italian sauce and was sure she would have appreciated all of the new vegan cheeses he had added to her pizza recipe.

Phoenix repositioned a basil leaf that was about to slide off the side of one of the steaming slices. Her dark eyes were bright with enthusiasm. On the day she had entered the doors of the foster group home she had thought her life was over. She believed she was destined to lead a miserable, institutionalized existence without the love and home she missed so much. Phoenix was glad she had held on. When she had written in her journal of the domestic violence tragedy in her home, she had thought things would never, ever get better.

Yes, she still had bad dreams sometimes and Phoenix did not trust people easily and some days were better than others. Yet, here she was, looking forward to the next challenge, to her next mission, planning ways to help others, both two-legged and four, and enjoying the company of her good friends.

She smiled to herself knowing that Midnight, the feline friend she had helped rescue, was curled up on her pillow, safe, and free from any harm. It was a comforting feeling knowing that Midnight was softly snoring in the room she shared with Vanetta. The night she had met Veganza and Courage had changed the trajectory of her life and now she gained energy and hope from helping others.

Phoenix still couldn't believe their band LIBERTY had a hit song "Free in the Sea." Who would have thought their video in front of the former sea prison would go viral after it was shared on social media accounts? The song happened to be released on the exact same day the captive orca was discovered in the Puget Sound sea pen by a Lummi Nation elder. This had assisted their song in its viral sensation trajectory and it was now up to 4 million views.

Phoenix marveled after they finished the rehearsal at the unexpected route life could take as she savored her melting but still oh so good chocolate raspberry shake. Here she was, not even fifteen yet, and so much had happened already. Who knew how successful the next strategic action plan created by the magical Veganza Animal Hero Crew could be?

"Hey, Phoenix, I heard you talking in the yard last night when I noticed you weren't in bed," said Vanetta. The group home teens in the band all knew about the existence of the Veganza Animal Heroes now and were each 100 percent behind their mission and could be trusted to keep quiet about it. The old saying "loose lips sink ships" was an adage they all subscribed to.

"We have another daring mission on the table. This time in daylight, if we choose to accept it." "Hmm… interesting," replied Rick. They each made sure their cell phone was turned off. The teens gathered closer around their big plate of shared pizza and their tall glasses of chocolate raspberry shakes. The tops of their heads almost touched as they whispered standing in a similar position to how the Veganza Animal Hero Crew had interacted the day before.

CHAPTER 8

Mercy

The black, fresh burn mark from the electroshock prod still stung as the mother pig tried to reach her baby with her nose through the bodies and feet of her porcine companions. The rattle and rumble of the transport truck moved forward through the night. The sun had risen and set three times since all of the pigs had been corraled and loaded using harsh handling and electroshock prodding. What fresh puzzling pain and fear faced the mother pig when the truck stopped, she had no idea. Her one surviving piglet tried to get close to her mother for sustenance and comfort.

The driver of the transport truck was just finishing his almond milk latte. His daughter had convinced him to switch from cow's milk to plant milk a month ago. He breathed so much clearer now and his skin looked healthier since he switched to veggie burgers instead of his former cow burgers. He heard the sound of hundreds of hooves scrape as they slid on the metal floor, through the back wall of his cab. It may be time to rethink taking these types of driving jobs. The more his daughter told him about the rich social life of pigs, the more uncomfortable he became with driving them to their certain, terrifying deaths. He could not let the factory farmers he picked the animals up from, the slaughterhouse workers or his truck driving colleagues know he felt a sense of sadness and hopeless mercy for his ill-fated passengers.

Freedom

To the human eye, it looked like an array of clouds were moving in a random pattern across the sky, morphing into varying shapes and different degrees of fluffiness. Covered by his day cloud adorned cape Freedom floated, enveloped and completely invisible to the human eye. He saw the stage was set below near the entrance to the slaughterhouse. The building sign proclaimed it was World Abattoirs, Quality Meat Packers. They were both misleading terms, like the word processing, thought Freedom.

Phoenix, Vanetta and Rick stood with other animal activists, some held white signs with different messages written in black marker. One stated, "Be an Animal Hero— Go Vegan!"

Phoenix held a water tank filled with fresh water. A tube was attached to the tank that was capable of spraying in between the holes of the transport trucks so the water could reach the extremely thirsty pigs. The activists could see the scorch marks and open wounds on the pigs and those who were more seriously injured, cowering at the back of the overcrowded slaughterhouse truck.

Phoenix sprayed some water towards a mother pig and her baby through the oval hole in the last section of the metal transport truck. The truck was confining

approximately two hundred miserable pigs. The majority of them had not yet reached six months of age. This is the average age that pigs are killed to satisfy an urge for a certain type of snack or meal. It is hard to fathom that every one of the 121 million pigs killed each year in the United States is an individual with their own distinct personality, like Lovey.

The air brakes made a hissing sound as the truck halted at the closed gate. Twenty or thirty years ago, there were no gates and high fences with barbed wire rolled at the top to keep animal cruelty investigators out. Today, the corporations who profit from the bodies of these animals knew they could not let the public see what goes on behind their walls. It would seriously affect their profit margins.

The stench from the slaughterhouse was thickly putrid. Phoenix stood with a crowd outside the slaughterhouse gates. She was ready to give water to the pigs through a long-tubed water spray nozzle that could reach through the openings to the dehydrated, stressed passengers. Phoenix was joined by activists who feel the same way she does about stopping the suffering of other animals.

The driver hesitated to leave the front cab of his truck to ring the bell, so, he leaned out of his open window and instead let loose the loud blare of his air horn. He saw a wispy beam of light begin to curl toward him. As he watched, the light shone pearlescent in a hypnotic swaying movement, encircling the truck. When he froze, his hand was still on the air horn switch and the truck engine idling had stopped. The pigs froze still and every human as well, except Phoenix and her two friends, Rick and Vanetta. Veganza's ivy-covered cane came into their eye view. The slow curls of light emanated from her cane.

Veganza's magnificent wings made a whooshing sound as Freedom and Veganza landed beside the truck driver's side door. "You are a baby pig. You were just born. You feel metal under your feet and your mother tries to protect you and your brothers and sisters from being trampled by the panicked feet of the other pigs. The truck rattles and heaves side to side as it drives forth. Your fellow pigs are packed in so close together that your mother cannot even lay down for you to drink her milk. You don't know there are such things as grass, a wide-open field or the sound of birds. Your mother has only seen the inside of an industrial sized metal shed. The fear in the truck is palpable, like a thick noxious blanket. You are puzzled as to why your mother is wounded. She can't reach you because of all of the overcrowded, petrified passengers crowding together. You wonder: Is this the end for me or the beginning?" whispered Veganza into the truck driver's ear.

Freedom lifts both of his arms up and outwards by the giant side wheels of the truck. Swirling around him fly a legion of crows, hawks, ospreys and pigeons. In a fast fluttering of wings, the birds place their different sized wings around the base of the truck. Freedom marshals the strength of the wind. "1,2,3, GO!" Freedom yelled. The truck lifted. The driver still slept on in the twilight of Veganza's frozen trance. There was not a sound from the passengers as they, too, were still under Veganza's spell. No one in the truck felt fear any longer as they slept like babies. The truck wheels lifted up higher from the ground. Phoenix, Vanetta and Rick were still surrounded by their motionless activist friends. They were part of a global movement called "Animal Save."

The three friends watched the truck be lifted up and away by a league of determined birds with Freedom at the helm. First, the truck gathered speed, upwards, so slowly, and then it lifted higher into the bright daylight of the sky. The other Animal Save activist friends began to wake from Veganza's spell. They saw the truck was no longer within their arms' reach. Everyone jumped for joy when they saw the receding truck getting smaller and smaller as it floated away into the clouds.

They grabbed their cell phones to record the unbelievable sight of a multitude of bird species with their variety of colored wings rescuing their relatives. They each began posting images and videos on their social media pages with headlines saying, "If I didn't see it with my own eyes" and "You're not going to believe this."

CHAPTER 9

Paradise

O nce again Courage greeted her fellow animal defenders at the shore. This time, she and her fellow sea creatures swarmed around a seaweed-covered craft shaped like a hovercraft. The pig passengers slept on, oblivious to their liberation. Their bodies began to heal as they rested. The truck driver, Michael Daniel, also slept, still in a frozen state, under Veganza's spell.

Freedom, Veganza and all of the birds propelled the transport truck forward onto the waiting seacraft. The water parted in a surf covered triangular shape as the sea creatures took over the job of liberating the still sleeping pigs from their feathered friends. Courage led the way. Veganza and Freedom flew above the entourage as they journeyed to paradise.

What is paradise for pigs you, the reader, might ask? If only you could see the reaction of the pigs as they woke from their deep sleep to hear the back doors opening. They

moved forward cautiously. They smelled fresh air and felt grass and sand on their hooves for the first time. Open gentle arms welcomed the pigs as they were fed fresh watermelon and drank clean water. Those who were injured were tended to. The mother pig and her piglet and all of their fellow former factory-farmed tribe knew they were home, safe at last. They had arrived at their form of paradise.

Michael Daniel, the truck driver, marveled at the scene when he woke up to see pigs walking in the cool, clean water, enjoying for the first time in their lives the feeling of being cared for by gentle hands rather than being punished by harmful hands. He knew this was the way they were all supposed to live, naturally, with their families, feeling the earth under their feet. He couldn't wait to let his daughter know his epiphany was now complete. He picked up his cell phone to tell her the fantastic tale.

Veganza and Freedom looked down at the happy scene from a cloud and gave the universal V for victory sign to Courage before she swam away with her sea friends back to her watery home in the sea caves in the deepest part of the ocean.

Progress

"Unbelievable videos posted today by animal activists went viral. They showed an entire transport truckload of pigs being lifted into the air by hundreds of birds! Some say the videos are doctored. We have in the studio with us today Anita Krajnc, founder of *Animal Save*. Anita, can you tell us were these videos doctored and, if they weren't, what in the world was going on?" intoned the CNN reporter. "We witnessed today, Anderson, a winged rebellion in action. Other animals came to the rescue of the most abused and ignored group of animals in the world, factory-farmed animals. I communicated with activists who were at the

Animal Save vigil at the slaughterhouse this morning and the videos they took are real. We are at a crossroads, Anderson. Other animals are rebelling at being treated so cruelly by us humans."

"What are you saying, Anita? Do you think the world is going to go vegan?"

"I am saying that a flying transport truckload of pigs lifted by the wings of hundreds of birds cannot be ignored. It is a clear message: We need to change how we treat our fellow animals. My colleague, Susan Hargreaves, with the kindness education project, *Be an Animal Hero*, reported to me that the free Veganza vegan tip sheet on their website has been viewed millions of times today. This is unprecedented."

"We are doing a CNN survey. Let us know what you think: Was this an apparition or reality? Will you change the way you eat after the video we all saw today?" asked Anderson.

The Journey Continues

Phoenix, Vanetta and Rick finished packing their musical instruments into the back of the black van. The band van was now emblazoned with stunning original artwork created by Monique Martinez showing the Veganza Animal Heroes in action. Ron, the group home counselor also doubled as the ethical and trustworthy manager for their band called LIBERTY. Phoenix had kissed the top of Midnight's feline head as she said goodbye before her trip this morning. She knew Irene would take good care of the cat she rescued, which had started her on this adventure.

The scenery sped by as the palm tree fronds waved in the breeze. She could feel the sun warming her head through the window. Phoenix reflected on her life. She still had the trauma of losing her mother reappearing once in a while as she tried to sleep. But when she helped others who had also suffered, two-legged or four, she felt effective and useful. She knew she would not be the person she is today if not for her history, both good and bad. Her past had fueled her empathy. Her present was full of adventure. She knew her future would be whatever she planned for and worked towards. One of the many things she learned from the Veganza Animal Hero Crew is that anything is possible.

Vegolution

"Today we are making Southern Vegan Cornbread, collards and black beans on "Vegan Feeds Your Soul". We are in the midst of a massive vegolution. The number of vegans has sky-rocketed since the truckload of pigs were sighted being rescued by all the creatures in the sky. It was a vision of liberation we will never forget, a clear message about how we treat farm animals," intoned chef Angela Means, from her television show on the cooking channel, which had evolved into an all-vegan food network. The network was responding to the latest figures that saw a 70% increase in people going vegan.

"Today, our musical guests, the band LIBERTY, are here with their new number one hit."

Colored spotlights shone on the three young musicians as their voices sang in harmony with the background of rhythmic, vibrating electric guitar chords being strummed by Rick.

You say you want a vegolution,
well, you know, we all need to change the world,
You tell me that it's evolution, well you know,
we really need to save the world,

And if you want money for destruction and hate,
all I can tell you is you have to wait,
you know vegan is alright, ALRIGHT!

The studio audience cheered as the three took their bows. Most of the audience had seen the miraculous truck-load of pigs flying in the air on the way to what they all knew would be a much better fate. The video had made them think, consider, research, ruminate and now they were all… you guessed it, vegan.

CHAPTER 10

Ireland

Jules' inky black wings flapped soundlessly over the treetops. The scene unfolded below him in a tumultuous, undulating river of green banyan leaves, whispering in the warm breeze.

He swooped down and landed on a leafy branch adorning Veganza's banyan tree home. An extended beak bent forward as Jules peered inside a space hollowed out inside the knot of the root-strewn trunk.

Veganza's glossy head of hair swung as she leaned in closely to her feathered friend's face. Jules explained what he had heard from the other creatures. He advised Veganza to make a speedy exit from her Everglades home and embark on an emergency journey across the sea.

"How old is your news, Jules?" queried Veganza.

Satisfied with his answer, her wings pointed in an upwards arc as she shot directly up and out through the top of the tree, holding Lovey in one arm, to start her journey across the sea.

A silvery blue tail reflected in the ocean below Veganza as she flew. A glossy head gleamed in the sunshine like a wet seal and rose above a wave. Courage waved her hand in greeting. "Jules heard the news. Mother is near the end of her 700-year life span. She needs me by her side," said Veganza. "I will lead you on the fastest route to the green mountains and valleys of Wicklow County. I can visit with the mermaid contingent on the other side of the ocean," replied Courage.

A cloud floated closer to Veganza and Lovey, "Hey, on your flight back to your native land, we can get there faster if you rest once in a while on my cloud," said Freedom.

The four friends progressed forward, Freedom on his cloud, Veganza and Lovey with her head tucked under Veganza's chin and Courage leading them over the sea.

It had been many years since Veganza had seen her biological family. The creatures she saw daily in the forest and her swimming and flying friends were now her extended family.

The Veganza Animal Hero Crew travelled swiftly. It helped to have powerful friends, like Freedom controlling the wind, and her sea friend Courage, navigating the most efficient route over the waves.

Up ahead, Veganza began to see the rock-strewn shore of the shining emerald Wicklow Mountains. The news had spread that the Veganza Animal Heroes were on their way. In the sheltered rock caves, a force of mermaids, dolphins, and seals swam towards Courage as she was the first of her fellow heroes to enter the bay.

Veganza landed on the pebbly sand with Freedom. Lovey enjoyed sniffing the new fresh smells. She had never been to Ireland before.

All of the mermaids, seals, and dolphins visited for a while sharing the lemon artichoke baked dish made in

honor of the visit of Freedom, Courage, Lovey and Veganza. They discussed, briefly, the changes they were seeing in the global treatment of other animals thanks to the remarkable headline grabbing adventures of Veganza, Freedom and Courage and the rest of their animal hero friends.

It was time for Veganza and Lovey to fly across the Wicklow Mountains, through the mists of the Avoca Valley and to her mother's bedside in the depths of the hidden forest. "Veganza, if you need me, you know you just have to call my name and I'll be here," said Freedom before returning to his floating home in the sky. His azure-colored cape flowed behind him. Courage called a goodbye to Veganza before diving under the inky sea.

CHAPTER 11

Matriarch

One of the tenets of the ancient matrilineal tradition of the animal hero tribes is that, after their life span of approximately seven hundred years, the mother passes to her eldest daughter the matriarchal crown. This is not an actual crown you can see, it's a mission, a continued determination, a crown that doesn't make anyone better than anyone else. It's an imaginary crown of thoughts, always considering the next strategic step. It's an ever-present sense of responsibility and dedicated caring for all of the animal heroes' work, their empowerment and challenges. Veganza was still relatively young in her seven hundred years life expectancy. She was only a hundred years old.

Veganza landed on the mossy ground in the mists of the Avoca Valley. Holding Lovey in the crook of her arm, she ducked through a sinewy wall of weeping willow branches and entered a private chamber protected by the densest forest on the Wicklow Way, in Ireland.

Her mother, Danu, lay on a soft, green bed of moss surrounded by a large circle of deer, fox, pine marten, otters, wild goats, badgers, red squirrels, Irish hares, rabbits, wood mice and hedgehogs. Connor, the Irish wolfhound, her mother's constant companion, lay his big soft head on Danu's arm. When Lovey approached, Connor stepped away from the mossy bed, momentarily, to greet Lovey, nose to nose.

As Veganza approached, her mother's eyes opened, unfocused at first. "You have returned at last." Her voice was a mere whisper of its former firm strong self. An Irish hare, one of the three species of rabbits living in Ireland, hopped over with a crystal glass of a green smoothy drink, full of vitamins, Irish sea moss and minerals. Danu sipped the refreshing drink with parched lips. Veganza placed her hand on top of her mother's hand. "My seven hundred years have been full of effective rescues and soothing beautiful nature." She swallowed hard. Speaking was an effort. "My matriarchal role draws to a close. I have not achieved my goal of a vegan Ireland. Vegan for the good of us all, the human and non-human animals, the land, the water and the air. I have discovered a way to enhance our powers though. I have left you the spell instructions in the Crystal Cave. You are ready to be the head matriarch when I pass."

Veganza, knowing the time was near, and respecting her mother's capable nature, replied truthfully, "I agree to take on my expected role. I will return to the Florida Everglades to help, periodically."

"I know the world changes and understand your wish for the wider world to be kinder to all animals. I have heard through the animal news of your adventures and progress. I was surprised and skeptical at your trust of the egocentric human species to selflessly help. You have succeeded in increasing the awareness of animal suffering in many people in the United States. This is no small feat. I regret I must leave you behind without reveling in the success and warmth of true animal liberation."

Her voice after such a great effort began to faulter to a whisper. "Please turn this green island truly green." These were the last words of Danu. All of the many species of earthlings surrounding her bed bowed their heads. They knew that death was a part of life, yet they still mourned the passing of their family member. Veganza lay the first leaf from the forest ground. Each forest creature joined her in the ritual of laying leaves on Danu's bed as was their ancient custom. They turned and walked silently and slowly back to their individual forest homes. Lovey sat still by Veganza's side. The sun was setting over the Wicklow Mountains. Veganza turned away from her mother and picked up Lovey and held her close in her arms. She gained such comfort from her constant, undemanding company. Connor gave Danu one last velvet muzzle kiss on her forehead and joined Veganza as he was instructed to do before she arrived. Danu will now slowly return to where she came from, the earth.

Tears ran in glistening rivulets from beneath her closed eyelids as Veganza walked past a weeping willow tree in Glendalough on the Wicklow Way. Connor, with his long-legged stride knew the way home. Veganza's life work was still before her. She decided to rest first in her native land before planning how she would achieve her mother's dying wish. It was a goal she would have set for herself, anyway. She could have flown but needed to walk, cloaked in the familiar sounds of her forest childhood.

Native Home

Veganza heard the whooshing, silvery sounds of rushing water before she opened her eyes surrounded by the aged stone wall. She peered up looking through the same hole in the craggy ceiling of rock she had gazed through for so many years.

Lovey, curled in the folds of Veganza's green velvet cape, appreciated its nest of warmth. Connor lay in his own bed made by Danu when he was found wandering in the Wicklow National Park as a pup, abandoned. All three greeted each other after rising.

Veganza began to search for the new spell her mother had whispered about yesterday as she lay struggling through her weakened breath. She had to find the spell she was working on. Veganza looked behind the base of the roots for a hidden scroll. Then she saw Connor moving the mossy pillow aside. It was the very pillow Veganza had slept on. Connor moved it with his long nose, and there it was, folded in a green velvet envelope, written on a parchment leaf.

Veganza held this possible key to achieving her mother's deathbed wish close as the three friends walked outside. Veganza and Connor had to duck under the natural low arch of the doorway disguised as solid rock behind the Powerscourt Waterfall. No human ever would have thought there was an opening behind the waterfall leading to their secret sanctuary. This hidden entry ensured a haven of safety, privacy and serenity.

Lined up on a sturdy branch of an 800-year-old oak tree were carefully chosen gifts of hazelnuts, a pot of blackcurrant jam, a small Irish brown loaf of bread and freshly picked mint leaves for tea. The creatures of the woods, those who flew, those who walked or climbed had each foraged and created this Irish breakfast bounty. Veganza opened the envelope and began to read her mother's graceful writing, intently.

She broke off pieces of bread and dipped them in the blackcurrant jam. She knew the best way to deal with their grief at this time was action. Veganza began to plan the first steps of her mission, rolling over the different possibilities in her mind while she read and chewed.

Greystones

The Irish coast in County Wicklow was known for its grey stones, a wild undulating line of uneven rocks. Veganza and Lovey flew over Greystones. The peach tinted sky shone gold on the ocean as Veganza landed by the shore. At this early hour, the beach was deserted except for two similar heads bobbing in the sea. Sheltered by an outcropping of rock, Veganza was hidden from the swimmers as they shook and jumped up and down reacting to the fresh, bracing sea breeze. The two fit brothers donned their warm, fluffy cotton robes and walked together, as they had done since they had learned to walk, identical heights and an identical length of step.

Veganza stepped out, surprising the twins. "Woah," they exclaimed simultaneously, "what manner of creature are you?"

"You have heard of me, and I have heard of you. I know you and your Happy Pear crew are helping to make Ireland truly green."

"Veganza!" said Steve. "Of course, who else could it be?" said Dave.

"Would you both consider helping to achieve a major veganizing milestone?" asked Veganza.

The brothers looked at each other for a millisecond. "We're in," said the Flynn brothers, characteristically in unison.

"I have enjoyed your Happy Pear podcast whenever I need a bit of a lift and...," began Veganza. The three figures sat sheltered from view in the same outcrop of rocks Veganza had appeared from earlier. The sunrise threw its remaining pinkish strands across the sky as the creative, determined planners plotted.

CHAPTER 12

Empathy

The green of Ireland gleamed in its Sunday best, the sparkle of the coastline its jewels. A giant pear tree mural painted on the side of a quaint whitewashed brick building served as the cheery backdrop for this podcast episode. Adjusting the camera direction behind the tripod stood Sara, a slender long-haired bolt of energy who led global social media campaigns, reaching millions. Darragh, another engaged Flynn sibling, who prefers to be behind the scenes, strategically positioned a sound boom off to the side.

"Today, as promised, we have a unique," said Dave, "unprecedented line up of surprise guests," said Steve. "This has never happened before. It's definitely unprecedented," agreed Dave.

"You may have heard stories of her before, and we have wondered ourselves," said Steve. "Is there really such a being?" finished Dave. The twins stepped aside to sit on top of one of the bleached wooden picnic tables in their outdoor dining area to watch the rest of the show unfold.

Veganza landed swiftly in front of the pear tree's painted trunk. Lovey sat in the crook of her arm, her magic, ivy-covered Irish blackthorn branch was held securely with the other hand. She silently pointed her curved cane and moon-colored tentacles curled forward. Cell phone screens wavered and crackled. Bam! Veganza appeared on every type of phone screen... every single type of phone device with a screen around the world—if it was turned on—revealed a cerulean blue-winged creature with a billowing, green velvet cape and an ancient-looking Lovey smiling in anticipation.

A collective gasp was heard around the world when people of all nations, of all ages, peered closer at their screen, watching and listening for what would come next. Veganza's cape fanned to the side. A small white chicken gingerly stepped forward. A light beige pink pig ambled her head from side to side as she joined her hen friend. Then a cow calmly took her time and stepped in front of the camera. She was followed by a young lamb who resembled Lovey. All six figures in front of the camera stood in silence. Sara, Darragh, Steve and Dave were as transfixed as the rest of the phone watching globe. They leaned forward, expectantly. The chicken, pig, cow and lamb opened their mouths and beak and started to speak in a language humans could understand.

In unison, their high and low timbered voices harmoniously rang out, emanating from every phone screen. Some people slept through their message or were going about their business without having their phone close by.

"We are each as individual as you, with our own unique personalities, like your companion dog or cat or horse, or anyone in your family. You and us, we are all animals. We experience joy, pain, comfort and fear, like you do. We all wish to live free from suffering. Will you discover the reality of our lives and our deaths?"

Then, Veganza raised her cane yet again and a sinewy trail of white smoke curled forward. Every viewer felt what each mother cow felt when her baby was taken away so people can drink the milk intended for her calf. Every viewer felt the fear of their fellow earthlings lining up for a fate they knew was an entrance to a final hell. Every single viewer of every age felt the bewilderment of the male chicks pecking out of their shells on conveyor belts only to be gassed right after hatching. In India, people lining up for curried roti stared at their phone screens. Every phone screen showed Veganza and her friends. In Australia and New Zealand, most people slept. In Brazil, people sitting in sports bars stared at their mobile phone screens while a soccer match played on large television screens. People sitting in steak restaurants watched their cell screens aghast. In Japan, in seafood restaurants, patrons watched their cell screens. Veganza and her animal friends were visible over the shoulders of people sitting on New York subways.

All of the viewers felt the last suffocating gasp of a fish caught in a net. People sat in restaurants with snow-covered mountain peaks in the distance, their gaze glued to their phones. In every country, every race, every religion, everywhere where there were cell screens being watched, each individual exchanged their own reality and experienced the feelings of their trapped, beleaguered, threatened, exploited, frightened, fellow beings. They awoke from Veganza's empathy fostering trance with so many questions, so many realizations.

Not everyone was persuaded, of course. Some were sleeping, some were working, some were in hospital, but it was the start of a global awakening, an epiphany for a lot of the world's population. It was an impossible-to-ignore shift in conscience for many people worldwide. Many individuals experienced a "veganiphany". This was one of Veganza's favorite words she had created. "Veganiphany" referred to an epiphany-type realization resulting in a person going vegan.

Then Veganza held her cane beside her again and the animals returned to the shelter of her cape. She waved to the Happy Pear Crew before shooting straight upwards into the sky, still holding Lovey in the crook of one arm. Darragh, Steve, Dave and Sarah, shielded their eyes as they looked into the bright sky as Veganza's form became smaller and smaller as she began her triumphant flight back to her Irish hideaway.

CHAPTER 13

Celebrate

Freedom loved this time of day just before the sun began to set. His bright sky-blue cape flowed through the amber lit clouds. He travelled surrounded by the magic.

He swooped down towards the San Juan Island cove, the same cove in which the world had witnessed the orca family reunion. The ripples in the water revealed a variety of moving tails, fins and shiny scales in animated movements. When Freedom landed, he realized the swirling just under the surface was the embodiment of joy and glee. Courage was there with her international mermaid crew, joined by legions of dolphins, seals, sea turtles—a veritable cavalcade of sea species, including the orca family whose home waters they were all reveling in.

"We're celebrating the victories of the end of captivity, less fishing, the end of the Japanese dolphin killings, the end of the Faroe Island pilot whale massacre, and the beginning of more life for us and the planet!" said Courage. "All the captive marine mammals are free. All captive wild-life have been returned to their native habitats."

"Yesss!! We are sprung!" squeaked a dolphin with the newly formed pod from the Miami Seaquarium, SeaWorld and all former captive sea "exhibits."

All heads nodded when Freedom said, "The global screen-saving action achieved a considerable increase in empathy! More of the world being vegan has stopped much animal exploitation and abuse. Fewer people are buying products that harm animals. Fewer humans are hunting or going to shows that harm animals. Empathy and awareness leading to action is the great changemaker."

"Will you take these crabless cakes to Veganza?" Courage gave a container of the savory cruelty-free treats to Freedom. Everyone waved their fins, feet and claws towards Freedom as he speedily soared away.

Miami Nice

Bubba, Khendall and his mother, Tara, walked towards the giant flashing sign from the parking lot overlooking Biscayne Bay. "Miami Wave Scene" the sign proclaimed. "Wow we are lucky to get tickets and a parking spot. It's jumping," said Tara with her southern twang. "We have very important connections," replied Bubba. "Awe, you guys, you know, every child and teen with the *Be an Animal Hero* crew received free tickets to the benefit concert to give Susan's kindness education books to schools and to pay for our youth empowering to compassionate action group home programs." "Sure is a long way of saying helping everyone," replied Bubba. Khendall wore a basketball shirt with the words "Be an Animal Hero" on the back. The trio gave in their tickets at the kiosk to the new wave park and concert venue on the former site of the Miami Seaquarium.

The owners had decided to move into a more sustainable and profitable business with a future.

Happy

Ron peeked through the black curtains, "Great turn out. What a crowd. I still haven't heard anything about our surprise guest for our first song though."

Chuck, the security guard, was now the head of the Miami Wave Scene security unit. You may recall, dear reader, that he was promised a job the night the LIBERTY band played to create a diversion for Lolita's liberation. Chuck said, "I just had word he has entered the grounds through the backstage area." He put his phone back in his uniform pocket.

"Alright, are we ready?" asked Phoenix, turning to her fellow band members. Phoenix and her band members now had enough money saved up to go to college. Phoenix had even started a scholarship and business seed start-up fund in her mother's name for group home teens to be dispersed by the *Be an Animal Hero* charity.

The stage door opened to reveal a figure wearing a tall tan derby hat. He stepped forward. "Pharrell, thank you so much for joining us for this vital cause," said Vanetta. "Yes," concurred the small crowd. "I bought a ticket for the green pair of vegan sneakers you donated," Rick shyly stated. "Happy to help," said Pharrell. "It's a wonderful world and time for the show," said Ron, doing his best Louis Armstrong impression. Phoenix, Rick and Vanetta all knew Ron was in a good mood when he spoke like Louis.

The curtains opened. The crowd roared doubly loud when they saw the LIBERTY band members and Pharrell raise their hands, simultaneously, in the V sign.

Vanetta started them off with a staggered drumbeat.

Phoenix, Vanetta, Rick and Pharrell all began to sing.

It ain't so crazy, what I'm about to say,
Kindness is here, bake a vegan cake,
I'm a freedom hero see this happy face,
Saving them, we're all family, every day,

Because I'm happy, clap along, when the world is vegan
like a room without a roof,
Because I'm happy, clap along, if you feel like kindness
is the truth,
Because I'm happy, clap along, if you know what
happiness is to you,
Because I'm happy, clap along, if you feel that's
what we want to do,

Here come good news, vegan's where it's at,
Give it all we got, don't hold it back,
I should probably warn you we'll be just fine,
No offense to you it's the end of killing time.

Everyone moved to the so easy-to-dance-to tune, all ages. Some jumped up to dance in the aisles, clapping along and moving to the music. Ron and Chuck joined in, too, off to the side of the stage. All in all, everyone was... you guessed it, happy.

CHAPTER 14

Evolve

A large metal transport truck pulled into the ferry loading area. Michael Daniel put the air brakes on to wait for the ferry. This time, his truck was filled with Beyond Meat burgers. The company had bought the old Quality Meat Packers slaughterhouse building. Ethan Brown, the founder of Beyond Meat needed to seriously increase his company's output production. The newly renovated building stood as a monument to positive change. Seth Tibbott, the founder of Turtle Island Foods, makers of Tofurky, had also bought every former slaughterhouse in Oregon and hired the former workers in response to the increased demand for his plant-based products.

Veganza, Freedom, Courage and their helpers had fast forwarded the natural evolution of the supply and demand food chain. The economic adaptation included Miyoko Schinner of Miyoko's Creamery buying up all of the former dairy farms. They also partnered with *Be an Animal Hero* to give free education programs.

Michael Daniel was looking forward to seeing his daughter, aptly named, Heart. She had started him on his journey to question how the world treats other animals. He could see the top of the eco-friendly tree house education center as he approached the shore. Heart, her cap of short hair shining, had a huge smile to greet her Dad. She was self-actualized, working at the sanctuary and education center. She woke up every morning with joy in her heart. Heart also loved designing creative store window displays for the empowering books Susan had written. "Susan is about to start her presentation about the politics of change to the Harvard honors class. They are going to love these Beyond Meat burgers," said Heart. "I brought some watermelon for Mercy. It's her favorite." "She's out with her daughter by the shore near the barn," replied Heart. "I am sautéing the onions now for the Beyond Meat burgers," said Chef Angela Means. She was donating her time to grill the burgers. She was a regular and very enthusiastic volunteer.

Michael Daniel sat with Mercy, giving her a belly rub. Mercy still remembered her ride to freedom. Now every day was filled with a natural, happy existence. Her daughter thought her life was always this way and didn't recall the horror of the truck driving to the slaughterhouse. The younger pig smacked her lips as she chomped down on the watermelon pieces, thoroughly enjoying the sweet, juicy treat. Michael Daniel marveled at the turn his life had taken. He never would have guessed in a million years that he would be sitting here enjoying the company of rescued pigs, never imagined he would be vegan and be a transporter for Beyond Meat. It just goes to show that you never know what's around the corner, thought Michael Daniel.

Celebration

Jules glided soundlessly on the updraft, his glossy feathers smooth as black marble. The towering pedunculate oak tree near the Powerscourt Waterfall was easy to spot, even from his ariel view.

Around the branch serving as a table sat a gathering of earthlings: deer, fox, pine marten, otters, wild goats, badgers, Irish hares, rabbits, wood mice and hedgehogs. Some crouched, some lay, lounged, sat or stood around the celebration feast. Freedom and Veganza, Lovey and Connor were enjoying the feast too.

Cast iron pans of roasted vegetables with jugs of gravy sat beside fresh green salads of dandelion greens and berries. Courage had sent along a pan of her crabless cakes with Freedom to contribute to the celebration feast.

The Irish red squirrels preferred to eat the acorns straight from the branch as did the pine martens.

The conversation was multi-layered. Varying sound levels rose up and down in tempo intermingled in a combination of excited bird noises and laughter. Periodically, Freedom's deep laugh could be heard.

Twinkling fairy lights began to pulse as the sun set on the feast. Jules tucked into a bowl of wild strawberries with his beak after greeting the throng, including his Irish cousins, the Jackdaw and the hooded crow.

Lovey sat on Veganza's knee, thoroughly enjoying the mood of the company, the overall sense of jubilation. She looked over at her newly adopted brother. Connor was nose to nose with a red deer as a blue butterfly landed on the top of the young fawn's head.

Veganza knew celebrations like this were concurrently happening in forests, woodlands, ocean coves, mountains, by streams, rivers and rainforests all over the Earth. She had heard the report by Hawkeye on the Animal Voices

News Service earlier. She knew Courage and all of her sea friends, including an international crew of mermaids, were reveling in the latest miraculous adventure of Veganza's animal heroes. She thought of her mother's now accomplished deathbed wish of a greener Ireland, growing into a burgeoning healthier, kinder and more sustainable economy. She knew there were still challenges ahead. After all, not everyone in the world was looking at a phone screen at the time she had tried out her mother's new spell. Veganza knew that she and her fellow animal heroes would be called on again to conquer more injustice.

Freedom caught Veganza's eye and raised his crystal goblet full of fresh blackcurrant juice. All the creatures raised their wings, paws, faces, and beaks up towards the night sky and were momentarily silent. "To life, freedom and our expanding multi-specied family."

Their cacophony of cheers could be heard above the rush of the Powerscourt Waterfall. Veganza sighed a breath of contentment. Then she leaned down and gave Lovey a kiss on the top of her head. Right now, she would revel in this sanctuary. Here, she would rest and revive until the next call for action needed to be answered by her relentless, high octane Animal Hero Crew.

The End

AFTERWORD

The character Veganza was morphed from the Mother Nature green caped storyteller character I created for early primary grades in my school presentations. I wrote a bonus short story at the back of *Animal Hero Kids – Voices for the Voiceless* in 2014 about a winged shero who lived in a banyan tree with the name of Saoirse. Do you know what Saoirse means? Well, that's why the name was changed to Veganza. Today, the world of Veganza has grown to include other heroes and is relatable for all ages. The short *Veganza Animal Hero* Claymation is also a delight.

The character of Phoenix is a blend of teens I have met in the foster group home system when I visit to present interactive programs in South Florida. A large majority of residents end up there due to their life being railroaded by incidents of domestic violence, addiction or other distressing circumstances. In my work visiting these residences, where I also provide free vegan food demonstrations, my heart goes out to these displaced young people. I marvel when they overcome their circumstances and stride forward as young adults following their dreams, like Phoenix did.

Freedom's character was inspired by vegan professional bodybuilder and great supporter of my empowering education work, Korin Sutton. Korin is always generous with his volunteer time and his easy sense of humor.

Courage the first ever vegan, brown mermaid super-hero character, was inspired by two real people, Angela Means and Kimaya Rao, both who courageously speak out, and make the world a kinder, more generous place. Angela is the real deal with her vegan soul food cooking and her big heart and Kimaya is one of the Animal Hero Crew and is featured along with all of the other Animal Hero Crew members in our online videos.

Khendall is also a real Animal Hero Crew member and speaks up for all animals not to be harmed.

At the time of the writing of this story, Lolita, the orca whale, was sick and possibly dying in her watery cell. I had just documented and witnessed, again, her misery, her form barely moving, trapped in the small tank. Since the mid-1980s, I have been protesting for her release from captivity. The Lummi Nation have a sea pen plan in her native waters and the local government in the San Juan Islands have been vocal about wanting her returned. It's possible by the time you read this, dear reader, she may finally be free from her watery prison. If she is, RIP Lolita, the formerly solitary orca prisoner.

Now, turn the page to start your journey to enjoy the scrumptious vegan recipes mentioned in the *Veganza Animal Heroes Series – Liberation* and a wealth of vital information about going vegan.

VEGAN RECIPES
featured throughout Veganza Animal Heroes – Liberation

Veganza's Ginger Spice Cake

Guaranteed to lift your spirits and fill your home with a comforting scent, this cake is best enjoyed with vegan butter and hot tea or coffee. Close your eyes and envision Veganza enjoying this vegan ginger spice cake in the interior of her banyan tree home when you take your first bite.

Ingredients

1 cup organic self-rising flour

1 tsp baking soda

1 tbsp ginger, a mix of fresh and ground

1 tsp cinnamon

1 tsp of vanilla

1 tsp mixed allspice

½ cup of dairy free margarine

½ cup of treacle or dark molasses

½ cup of golden syrup or maple syrup (Note: easy to make less sweet to taste by reducing the amount of syrup a little)

1 cup of dairy free milk (I like soy milk, some prefer oat milk or almond milk)

Instructions

1. Preheat your oven to 350 degrees Fahrenheit.
2. Grease a 9" loaf pan and line it with parchment paper or grease the pan and sprinkle a little flour. Parchment paper does work better and looks so homemade.
3. In a large bowl, mix together the flour, baking soda and spices.
4. In a saucepan, put the margarine, treacle, golden syrup and milk. Warm gently until combined and then add the mixture to the flour mixture.
5. Stir well with a large whisk until the mixture is smooth. However, the longer you stir it, the more likely it will end up tougher.
6. Pour the runny mixture into the lined loaf pan.
7. Bake for 55 minutes or until a fork or skewer put in the center of the cake comes out clean.
8. Leave the cake to cool in the loaf pan before turning it out.

Goes well with vegan butter and thick dark orange marmalade.

Scramble Fried Tofu

This recipe has been a staple in my life since 1980. I have modified it to add a bit of *Just Egg*. When I was 9 years old, I was taken to a hatchery and saw what they do to all of the male chicks. I find it so easy to live without eggs and let others live at the same time.

One of the wonderful things about tofu, apart from no animals being harmed, is that it takes on the taste of whatever you combine it with. There are so many egg substitutes on the market today. I never measure ingredients when I cook, but for you, dear reader, I will endeavor to list the measurements accurately. I love this tofu dish with burnt toast (the entire family is the same regarding the burnt toast thing) and brown HP sauce.

Ingredients

2–3 cloves of garlic, chopped
½ an onion, chopped
½ a tsp of curry powder
½ a tsp of savory sage or Italian seasoning
3 tbsp of nutritional yeast
a dash of *Braggs Amino Acids*
a sprinkling of black pepper, freshly ground
2 tbsp of vegan butter or olive oil

1 block of extra firm organic tofu
4 ounces of *Just Egg* (if you can't get an egg replacer product like this, it's no biggie, scramble fried tofu is still good on its own)
Finely cut broccoli florets, kale, green onions and sweet orange peppers. All together making up about half to ¾ of a cup.

Instructions

1. Sauté garlic and onion on low to medium heat in a non-stick frying pan in olive oil or vegan butter. Add the herbs and spices. Sprinkle some of the nutritional yeast. Add the mixture of veggies, except the green onions.
2. When it smells good, take the block of tofu after squeezing the water out of it, and crumble it into the frying pan. Add a dash of *Braggs* and fresh black pepper. Then mix, turn, stir, as it begins to brown.

Take a little taste and decide if you need to sprinkle any more herbs or spices and add the rest of the nutritional yeast and the green onions. Stir some more. Check to see if you have to add a little more vegan butter or a touch of olive oil.

3. Add the *Just Egg*. Taste one more time. Need to add anything? Then stir until the fried tofu is fluffy and browned.

You can enjoy scramble fried tofu with *Batchelors* or *Heinz* canned beans in tomato sauce, vegan sausages or vegan bacon, toast and tomato slices. If you have any leftover, it's good for making vegan fried rice or lasagna, too.

Phoenix's Chocolate Raspberry Shake

Chocolate and raspberries are a match made in heaven. The thickness of this shake can be controlled by the frozen banana and plant milk ratio. This is an afternoon pick me up good for you, the animals and the planet. Frost a goblet in the freezer and garnish with a raspberry chocolate wafer.

Ingredients

1 cup of vegan chocolate
   ice cream
½ cup of organic raspberries

½ to ¾ cup of vanilla soymilk
   or almond milk
½ of a frozen banana

Instructions

Blend and guzzle until you get a brain freeze!

Tri-Fecta Cheeza Pizza

Did you know that grocery store bakeries, or just regular independent bakeries, sell pizza dough that's accidently vegan and fairly inexpensive?

It's so easy to break apart, roll and put on a greased baking sheet.

So many vegan cheeses, so little time. Pick your favorite vegan cheeses: *Daiya Cheddar Cheese* slices cut into smaller pieces, *Miyoko's Mozzarella, Follow Your Heart Smoked Gouda* and you can make your own cashew cheese. All you need is a blender.

Pre-heat oven to 450 degrees Fahrenheit.

Cashew Cheese Ingredients

1 tsp of garlic powder	4 tbsp of nutritional yeast
¾ tsp of salt	½ cup of cashews
½ tsp of white pepper	¼ cup of tapioca flour

Instructions

1. Blend all ingredients fully.
2. On low heat in a non-stick pan, slowly heat and stir the liquid when it thickens.
3. Spread your favorite sauce. Add cashew paste in dollops and squish, sprinkle any of your no-cows-were-harmed or had-their-babies-taken-away for these cheeses.
4. Bake 12 minutes (depending on how thin you make the crust) at 450 degrees Fahrenheit.
5. If you have fresh basil leaves or fresh oregano, sprinkle a little on the pizza at the end.

Courage the Mermaid's Stuffed Shells

Courage loves serving this vegan staple. It's great with vegan Cesar salad, sautéed kale or collards on the side. The creator of this recipe, Ann Wiley, tells a story about two young male teens who were scoffing at the idea of a completely vegan catered event. They made a show of putting two of the stuffed shells on their plate, only. Fast forward five minutes and they were back asking if they could take the entire serving pan to their table.

Ingredients

20 or so jumbo pasta shells
1 tbsp Bragg's Amino Acids
3+ tbsp olive oil
4 cloves garlic, chopped
½ red onion, chopped
2 heaping tbsp of mellow white miso

2 heaping tbsp of toasted tahini
2 pounds of firm tofu
cold water
your favorite tomato sauce
(enough to top the 20 or so
jumbo pasta shells)

Instructions

1. Cook 20 or so jumbo pasta shells until al dente.
2. Sauté all other ingredients over medium/high heat, until soft (about 5 minutes).
3. Rinse 2 pounds of firm tofu, drain and break into small pieces in a bowl. Add 2 heaping tbsp of both mellow white miso and toasted tahini. You may wish to add more to taste. Mash well with a potato masher, leaving NO lumps. You want a nutty, cheesy, creamy consistency and taste. You may need to add a TAD more water to achieve the right consistency.
4. Mix the onion mixture in with the tofu and stuff this combined mixture generously into the pasta shells. Spoon your favorite tomato sauce over each shell. I use Prego Vegetable and thin it with water (about ⅔ Prego, ⅓ water, so it is not so acidic and less thick).
5. Bake uncovered at 350 degrees Fahrenheit for 20 minutes or until hot.

These stuffed shells are also great cold the next day.

   Thank you to Ann Wiley from South Florida for contributing her delicious recipe.

Mermaid Save-the-Sea Crabless Cakes

Courage and all of her sea friends are aware of how important it is to save the sea and the sea's creatures. Erin Fontes is a magician in the kitchen. She created this signature dish using the authentic OLD BAY seasoning mix. It's as impressive as it is delicious.

Ingredients

2 16 oz cans of artichoke hearts, roughly chopped
2 16 oz cans of heart of palm, roughly chopped
2 cups of gluten-free breadcrumbs
4 tbs vegan mayonnaise
2 white onions, minced
8 cloves garlic, minced
juice of 1 lemon

zest of 1 lemon
vegetable oil (enough to fry cakes)
1 tbsp OLD BAY seasoning
1 tbsp fresh thyme
salt and pepper to taste

For serving (optional):
slices of lemon, fresh arugula

Instructions

1. Heat 1 tbsp of olive oil in frying pan on medium.
2. Sauté the onions and garlic in the until they are slightly caramelized.
3. Add thyme, salt and pepper to taste. Set aside.
4. Mix together the artichoke hearts, heart of palm, breadcrumbs, lemon juice and zest and seasoning in a bowl.
5. Once the onions have cooled, add them to the bowl and mix. Set aside for 30 minutes.
6. After 30 minutes, form the mixture into small cakes and set them on parchment paper.
7. Best to cool the cakes overnight.
8. To cook: Either bake the cakes at 350 degrees Fahrenheit for 45–60 minutes or fry them in vegetable oil until they are golden brown.
9. Serve the crabless cakes with a slice of lemon on a bed of fresh arugula with avocado aioli (avocado aioli recipe to follow).

Avocado Aioli

Ingredients

2–3 ripe organic avocados
1 bunch of fresh organic cilantro
3–4 cloves of organic garlic
2 tbsp of organic lemon juice

2 tbsp of organic olive oil
2 tbsp of vegan mayonnaise
½ tsp of salt (to taste)
1 tsp of black pepper

Instructions

1. Mix all the ingredients together in a medium size bowl.
2. Serve immediately.

Thank you to Erin Fontes from South Florida for creating this marvelous recipe. I have had the good fortune to enjoy it a few times.

Southern Vegan Cornbread

If you don't have a cast iron skillet for this recipe, it's worth it to run out and get one. You can use it for the Roasted Veggies recipe on page 110 as well. Trust me, you will use it again and again. If you have ever watched the film *Fried Green Tomatoes*, you know how handy it is to have a cast iron skillet in the house. The queen of southern vegan cooking is hands down Chef Angela Means, the owner of the Jackfruit Cafe in L.A. You may recognize her name from the cult classic film *Friday* and this iconic phrase that stemmed from her role in that film, "Bye Felicia." Here is my version of vegan cornbread.

Ingredients

1½ cups (360 ml) creamy oat milk**
2 tsp apple cider vinegar
1½ cups (195 g) stone-ground yellow or white cornmeal (medium grind is my preference)
¾ cup (94 g) all-purpose flour
1 tbsp baking powder
½ tsp sea salt
4 tbsp (56 g) vegan butter, melted + 2 tbsp for greasing the skillet
¼ cup (56 mL) extra virgin olive oil or neutral-flavored oil of choice

¼ cup (40 g) organic brown sugar or a little less
¼ cup (84 mL) agave nectar
1 heaping tbsp of finely chopped rosemary (4 g)

For serving (optional):
softened vegan butter OR maple butter: 2 tbsp vegan butter with maple syrup to taste

Instructions

1. Preheat the oven to 400 degrees Fahrenheit and arrange a middle rack in the oven. Stir the vinegar into the oat milk and set aside for 5–10 minutes to slightly curdle.
2. In a large bowl, combine the flour, cornmeal, baking powder and salt. Whisk well to break up any clumps.
3. Make a well in the center and pour in the 4 tbsp melted vegan butter, oil, brown sugar, agave and buttermilk. Gently mix with a whisk until just smooth, taking care to not overmix – there will be lumps, that's okay!

4. Fold in the rosemary using a silicone spatula. Allow the batter to rest for 10 minutes, or up to 1 hour. It should look somewhat like a pancake batter.
5. Meanwhile, transfer a 9" or 10" cast iron skillet to the pre-heated oven to heat up for 10 minutes. Remove the pan from the oven (use oven mitts!) and add the 2 tbsp of vegan butter to grease the skillet. It will start melting almost immediately. Dust the pan lightly with a sprinkle of cornmeal, about 1 tsp.
6. Pour the cornbread batter into the hot skillet (but not too quickly or the butter will pool up to the top). Bake for 25 to 28 minutes (check at 25 minutes), until a toothpick inserted in the center comes out clean and the top is golden brown.
7. Transfer to a wire rack and allow to cool for 15 to 20 minutes before slicing. Serve warm, and with a pat of softened vegan butter on top of each slice, if desired.

**You can simply add 2 tbsp of melted vegan butter to 1½ cups of regular oat milk or soy milk to make creamy oat or soy milk. Another option is to use 1 cup of regular oat or soy milk and add ½ cup of Silk Coffee Creamer.

Lemon Artichoke Bake by Courage

How does Courage find the time to liberate animals and create these types of innovative recipes? I love chewing on the slightly charred baked lemon slices in this recipe. This is also good over organic angel hair pasta, tossed. It's great with soup and rosemary sprigs to garnish for help-yourself dinner parties. This dish can be an accompaniment or a main dish.

Ingredients

4–6 tbsp olive oil

two 14–15 oz. cans artichoke hearts (halved preferred)

1–1½ cups vegan breadcrumbs

1–1½ cups vegan Parmesan cheese

4–6 cloves organic garlic, thinly sliced

salt and pepper to taste

zest of 1 lemon

juice of ½ lemon

4–5 fresh rosemary sprigs

Instructions

1. Preheat oven to 375 degrees Fahrenheit.
2. Drain artichoke hearts (paper towels work best).
3. Pour 1–2 tbsp olive oil in saucepan over low to medium heat. Cook artichoke hearts until some browning occurs and set aside (being careful not to burn the artichokes).
4. Drizzle approximately 2 tbsp of olive oil in the bottom of 13" x 9" baking pan. Mix in roughly ¼ of the breadcrumbs (more/less to taste). Add salt and pepper to taste and spread the mixture evenly over the bottom of the pan (not too thick but just enough for a base for the artichokes).
5. Place sautéed artichokes side by side over the breadcrumb base. Place sliced garlic over the artichoke layer (more/less garlic to taste). Sprinkle the breadcrumbs, vegan Parmesan cheese and salt and pepper to taste over the artichokes/garlic layer (not too thick). Drizzle olive oil over the layer, being careful not to saturate it. Cover with a second layer of the sautéed artichokes and sliced garlic. Again, sprinkle breadcrumbs, vegan Parmesan cheese, salt and pepper to taste and olive oil. Repeat until all the artichokes are used up (could

be 2–3 layers). Feel free to add more cheese on the top layer as it will brown nicely when broiled.

6. Place very thin slices of lemon over the breadcrumb/cheese top (space lemon slices apart). Drizzle the juice from ½ lemon over the top. Drizzle olive oil over the top. Place whole rosemary sprigs over the top (4 to 5).

7. Cover with foil and place in the oven for 30 mins. Remove the foil and broil just until slightly browned. Serve with or without the lemon slices, depending on taste. The rosemary sprigs can be placed on the plate as decoration, if desired.

Kale & Blueberry Smoothie

In the *Veganza Animal Heroes – Liberation* story, Danu, Veganza's mother was given this smoothie by an Irish hare. I like it with more blueberries than most people. They are full of antioxidants and are high in fiber. Measurements vary depending on how many people you are making this for. I will list the recipe ingredients and quantities for two people.

Ingredients

One frozen banana (time saving tip: cut bananas or break into smaller pieces before freezing)
½ cup of frozen blueberries
¾ cup of fresh kale

Vanilla unsweetened oat milk, soy milk or almond milk (whichever plant-based milk you prefer)

Instructions

Blend. Enjoy!

Irish Brown Bread Mini Loaves

In Ireland, they have the best brown soda bread! Their whole meal flour is part of why it's so good. In the United States, we can add toasted wheat germ to the bread to help mimic the flavor. This is a dense bread.

Ingredients

1¼ cups of organic unbleached flour, self-rising (save a little flour for sprinkling)

1 cup organic whole wheat flour

½ cup of rolled organic oats

¼ cup of toasted wheat germ

1¼ tsp of baking soda

½ tsp of salt

4 tbsp of cold vegan butter

1⅓ cups of vegan buttermilk (easy to create by melting a little vegan butter in soymilk or using a little vegan creamer in your plant milk, I added about a ⅓ of a cup of pumpkin spice creamer to plain soymilk)

Instructions

1. Preheat the oven to 425 degrees Fahrenheit.
2. Lightly grease a baking sheet and then dust with flour.
3. In a large bowl, mix all dry ingredients thoroughly.
4. Using the tips of your fingers, crumble the butter into the bowl of dry ingredients until it all looks like big breadcrumb shapes and all ingredients are evenly incorporated.
5. Stir in the plant milk until blended. Turn the dough onto a lightly floured surface and knead for 30 seconds.
6. Sprinkle on more flour as needed to prevent sticking, yet, let the dough stay soft.
7. Roll the dough with your fingers into small ovals or balls. Put them on the baking sheet and lightly flatten. Lightly spread a little flour over the mini loaves with your hand and cut an X in the middle with a sharp knife.
8. Bake for 30 minutes, then cool on a wire rack for an hour and a half before slicing.

Roasted Veggies with the Best Gravy in the World

Grab the cast iron skillet you ran out to get to make the *Southern Vegan Cornbread* on page 104. I love one pot cooking. It's so easy on the dishwasher's hands. Seasonal celebrations with nut roast, *Gardein*, *Tofurky* or *Field Roast* goodies and this savory gravy on mashed potatoes are sublime. Try these Roasted Veggies with *The Best Gravy in the World* at Thanksgiving. Your guests will thank you!

Ingredients

1–2 packages fresh Brussel sprouts, trimmed and halved

1 large onion, diced

2 cups fresh kale, chopped

4–5 medium potatoes, cut in 1" cubes

2–3 large carrots, cut in 1" coins

4–6 large garlic cloves (more to taste), mashed

4–6 tbsp olive oil

2 tsp fresh rosemary leaves (dry if fresh is unavailable)

salt and pepper to taste

garlic powder to taste

nutritional yeast to taste

Instructions

1. Preheat the oven to 375 degrees Fahrenheit.
2. Place all the vegetables, including the mashed garlic cloves, into a 13" x 9" baking pan (preferably copper or ceramic) or cast-iron skillet. Cover evenly with olive oil. Add rosemary leaves and season generously with salt, pepper, garlic powder and nutritional yeast. Stir thoroughly for even coverage. Cover the baking pan with aluminum foil and place it in the oven for 50–55 minutes.
3. Remove the baking pan from the oven. Remove the foil. Stir the ingredients and top generously with nutritional yeast.
4. Return the baking pan or cast-iron skillet to the oven and broil until slightly browned.
5. Dish out roasted veggies into individual soup/stew bowls or add a veggie burger or vegan cutlet on the side.
6. Top with *The Best Gravy in the World* (recipe to follow). Enjoy!

The Best Gravy in the World

Ingredients

½ cup of vegan butter
organic all-purpose flour
boiling water

1 tbsp *Marmite/Vegemite*
1 tbsp browning seasoning
    liquid (like *Kitchen Bouquet*)

Instructions

1. In a frying pan or saucepan, cast iron or non-stick, stir ½ cup of vegan butter (preferably salted) until it melts, on low to medium heat.
2. Stir in enough organic all-purpose flour to make a paste (roux). Slowly add enough boiling water to cover the mixture thoroughly and stir with a whisk.
3. Dissolve 1 tbsp of *Marmite/Vegemite* into the mixture.
4. Keep stirring the gravy throughout.
5. Add 1 tbsp of browning seasoning liquid like *Kitchen Bouquet*.

Why Vegan?

"The most violent weapon on earth is the table fork."

—Mahatma Gandhi

VEGAN FOR THE ANIMALS

The stockyards at Keele Street and St. Clair Avenue in Toronto were an assault on the senses. The smell of fear was palpable. The electroshock-prodded animals being bullied down the truck ramps were terrified and confused. Their eyes were stretched wide enough to see the stripe of white at the sides.

I walked briskly with my head and gaze forced straight ahead wondering if I could keep it together and not let on how I really felt being in this hellish place. Men whipped, yelled and bullied young calves into the auction ring. They continuously hit them to keep the panicked calves moving as people bid on their lives. Every one of the animals' fates loomed, lethally.

A thin, panicked goat seemed to sense in me a friendly soul and stood straight up calling to me over her bars. A loud bleating seemed to me to be saying "Help, help." I was posing as an agricultural student doing a class project. I was holding a camera. I was a young-looking 23 years of age.

The person who worked at the stockyards was busy telling me the animals had not had water for two days as the water wasn't working. I knew this meant that the animals who were transported for days and who were now waiting to be bought and subsequently slaughtered had not eaten or drank for a long time. Some may say this was the least of their worries. I looked around at the hundreds of animals who were so obviously confused and searching for help. Some stood in the dusty water troughs. The man pushed them aside roughly to demonstrate that the faucet didn't work. I had to quell my natural urge to escape with as many victims of the animal agriculture industry as I could fit into my van. However, I was there to document the atrocities in order to expose the constant abuse and neglect the animals suffer.

Sir Paul McCartney has a quote about what would happen if slaughterhouses had glass walls. Have you seen, dear reader, what does happen behind the cement walls of slaughterhouses? Perhaps you have seen an undercover investigation video and thought, surely, it is not really that cruel at every factory farm, on every transport truck, in every stockyard or slaughterhouse?

It is not coincidental that so many egregious animal abuse cases have been documented again and again. How do you kill someone who doesn't want to be killed?

Worldwide, more than 70 billion land animals are killed by the animal-based agriculture industry and up to 2.74 trillion fish. When I think of those individuals, each one with their own distinct personality, with their own fear and capacity for happiness and joy, I envision each one as a someone like Lovey, my constant twenty-two-year-old canine companion. Every being has the capacity to enjoy their natural life. Do they deserve to have their lives taken from them for the sake of a meal or a snack?

A CHICK'S STORY

One year, when I worked at a wildlife rehabilitation center, someone brought in a wet, barely alive chick. We surmised that the chick was somehow separated from the mother chicken near the Fort Lauderdale airport where a brood of hens had escaped from one of the planes. When a very young animal is orphaned, they often need a form of warm, physical comfort to survive. In one earlier instance, we had even bonded a chick with a mother duck and her ducklings. The one big happy family swam in the rehabilitation center pool with the chick sitting high up on the mother duck, keeping dry and away from the water.

However, there was no non-human mom to bond her to at this time, so, after drying off the little, weak chick, I held her close to my heartbeat under my shirt, a common practice. The little chick came home with me and stayed in our bathroom at night away from the feline family members. With a heating pad turned down low, the chick nestled on a layer of towels. Whenever I went in to sit with and visit the little chick, he would climb up and fall asleep under my neck, curled up, completely trusting and content. When another chicken came in about his size, they enjoyed each other's company and they enjoyed having the space to stretch their growing wings. Their enclosure had soft sand. They quickly kicked up the sand causing little showers of dust. This is how chickens have what is called a dust bath. So, eventually, the little chick who had become a foster family member started to live with his own kind. He was very fortunate to be able to do all the natural things at a wildlife center that these friendly, gentle, inquisitive birds love to do.

The chick I had come to know and care for had his own individual personality. Chickens are the number one abused and ignored animals in the world.

We are All Animals

Every individual is a someone.

*We are at a tipping point in our cruel,
destructive treatment of the natural world
and all of the other animals on the earth.*

*We have separated ourselves, we have subjugated,
killed, harmed, hunted, beaten, separated their
families, poisoned, burned, electroshocked, jailed,
caged, tanked and eaten every other species
whether they fly, crawl, swim, slither or run.*

*We all can choose to help or aid other
animals rather than hurt and kill them
or pay others to kill them for us.*

*We can all choose empathy and compassion
over oppression, exploitation and apathy.*

We are all animals.

Source: susanhargreaves.com

VEGAN FOR THE EARTH

"I am here to say, our house is on fire."
—Greta Thunberg

We are in the throes of a climate crisis, a polar ice melting, flooding, on fire, natural disaster not waiting to happen situation. The United Nations 2021 report on climate change issued a "code red." They stated "A major opportunity for mitigating and adapting climate change..." is adopting plant-based diets. "A vegan diet is probably the single, biggest way to reduce your impact on planet Earth, not just greenhouse gases, but global acidification, eutrophication, land use and water use," stated the lead researcher, Oxford University's Joseph Poore. "It is far bigger than cutting down your flights or buying an electric car," he said.

"Cattle ranching, responsible for the great majority of deforestation in the Amazon, is pushing the forest to the edge of what scientists warn could be a vast and irreversible dieback that claims much of the biome," stated the Washington Post. "The United States bought more than 320 million pounds of Brazilian beef last year (2021) and is on pace to purchase nearly twice as much this year," continued Washington Post reporters.

Eighty percent of the world's farmland is used to raise farmed animals, the Oxford study states. The number of people we can feed by eating grains and vegetables and fruits compared with eating animals is far greater. Beef production uses 36 times more land than the production of peas, to give just one example. Vegancalculator.com calculates how much land, air and how many animals... you save by adopting a vegan diet.

VEGAN FOR HEALTH

A healthy balanced, vegan diet provides all the nutrients you need. This means consuming whole foods including vegetables, grains, fruits and nuts. People who eat vegan get more antioxidants, fibre, potassium, nutrients and vitamin A, C and E than people eating a more traditional diet.

The Academy of Nutrition and Dietetics says that vegans are less likely to develop heart disease, cancer, diabetes and high blood pressure.

The documentary *What the Health* and *The Game Changers* demonstrate clearly why more athletes and people who care about their health are choosing to eat a plant-based diet.

Vegan athletes excel on a vegan diet, and the global list is growing, exponentially. Lewis Hamilton, Venus Williams, Kyrie Irving, Colin Kaepernick, Dotsie Bausch, John Salley and Carl Lewis are all vegan athletes. Dave Scott, the only person to win the ironman triathlon six times was a vegan from 1980 to 1987.

Vegan diets also help keep skin clear and healthy. A group of 6,000 physicians form the Physicians Committee for Responsible Medicine. PCRM.org offers a wealth of information about healthy vegan nutrition.

Veganza's Vegan Tips:

Replacing Animal Products

THREE EASY STEPS TO GO VEGAN

"You can be an animal hero every day, every time you shop and every time you eat by choosing scrumptious vegan fare," says Veganza.

"So many beings are helped when you consume food without a history of suffering," says Courage, the mermaid.

"It's so easy today," says the author of the *Veganza Animal Heroes Series* and founder of Animal Hero Kids, Susan Hargreaves. She went vegan over four decades ago after investigating how animals on factory farms, on transport trucks, in stockyards and in slaughterhouses are really treated.

REPLACE ANIMAL PRODUCTS WITH PLANT-BASED PRODUCTS

"Anything you can do, I can do vegan," say many of the Animal Hero Crew members.

Today, this is a statement of fact. Good news, you don't have to live without scrumptious tastes and those comfort foods you are accustomed to. You can simply replace them.

Replace milk made by cow mothers for their calves with almond milk, soy milk, rice milk, oat milk, coconut milk, cashew milk, hemp milk... There are so many good-tasting plant-based milks on the market now.

Did you know?

Baby cows are taken away from their mothers so that humans can sell and buy the milk the cow mother made for her baby? Male calves are confined, isolated and fed iron deficient formula and then killed at 16–18 weeks of age to be sold and slaughtered for "veal." Sometimes, they are sent to slaughter even sooner if the dairy farm finds it's more profitable.

Humans are mammals and so are cows and raccoons. How do we know we are mammals? We, human animals, give our babies our own breastmilk when our babies are born. There is no reason one mammal species should drink the breastmilk from another mammal species. This breastmilk is specifically geared towards feeding their own young. A human mother's milk is perfectly formulated (by nature) to feed a growing baby human. In the same way, a cow mother's milk is perfectly formulated (by nature) to feed a growing calf. And the same for whales and mice and dogs and... you get the picture! All mammal species breastfeed their young with their own specific milk, which is perfectly formulated (by nature) for their own growing young.

Business Wire news predicts plant-based milk sales will surpass 21.52 billion dollars in 2024. Oat milk sales jumped by 686 percent in one year.

Veganza, the animal hero, likes vanilla soy milk in her cereal in the morning. Many adults like almond milk for their lattes. Oat milk is fast becoming many people's choice for hot chocolate and smoothies. Chocolate soy milk poured over frozen strawberries is an easy and delicious frozen treat. Check out Lovey's strawberry milk shake recipe in the *Veganza Animal Hero* picture book recipe section.

Happy Cow Cheese Is Vegan

You may have seen advertising about happy cows? The truth is the happy cows are the ones who are saved from having their babies taken away or being milked by machines. Happy cows live on real farm animal sanctuaries, where they enjoy doing all the natural things cows like to do.

There have been dramatic and delicious advances made in the area of vegan cheese over the past 30+ years. It now tastes great and it melts! There are also many different options available.

So why not replace cow-milk cheese and cheese products with vegan cheeses?

A few of the vegan cheeses you should definitely try:

- *Daiya Cheddar Cheese* slices: really good in grilled cheese sandwiches
- *Miyoko's Artisan* garlic and herb
- *Tofutti Better Than Cream Cheese*
- *Follow Your Heart* smoked gouda
- *Kite Hill* cream cheese and chive flavor
- *Earth Island Vegan Gourmet* cheddar and mozzarella cheese slices are good, too

There are so many choices nowadays that whether you are looking for Parmesan cheese, goat cheese, blue cheese or Feta... you name it, a vegan version (or many) already exists.

In many recipes, on popcorn and in pasta, nutritional yeast creates a cheesy tangy taste similar to Parmesan cheese.

Any recipe that calls for cow-milk cheese (think pizza, lasagna, macaroni and cheese, fondue, grilled cheese sandwiches, quiche, omelets, and any other cheese-based recipe you can think of) can easily be made using one or more of the scrumptious vegan cheeses now readily available on the market at health food stores and at larger grocery store chains.

No More Meat: Beyond Eating Animals

Tastebud-pleasing foods available by *Beyond Meat, Impossible, Turtle Island Foods (Tofurky), Gimme Lean* and *Gardein* are just a few of the compassionate meat replacement choices for your table. You will not be disappointed.

When Susan Hargreaves presents animal abuse investigation workshops for police, firefighters and animal control officers, the only complaint she ever received about the workshops is regarding the vegan lunch. But not in the way you might think! The officers kept accusing each other of taking too many *Gardein Crispy Tenders* in the lunch line... and everybody wants more, more, more!

Beyond Eating Eggs

I think that even the average North American has seen or knows about the conditions of chickens/hens/chicks on factory farms. Why not move beyond eating eggs and help society move away from these chicken prisons where they have no space, no natural sunlight, where they can't be with each other in natural family groupings, where they can't be with their young... where their lives are daily torture until they are killed. Your morning scrambled eggs do not have to rely on this cruel and unhealthy industry.

Try the *Scramble Fried Tofu* recipe on page 97. You have the choice of adding in some *Just Egg* if you're in the United States. This is optional, but I find that ¼ *Just Egg* and ¾ *Scramble Fried Tofu* is a perfect combination!

Just Egg has released a new product called folded egg. This is fabulous sautéed with a vegan sausage patty and HP sauce on a bun.

Egg Replacements in the United Kingdom, Ireland and Australia

If you are in the UK, *Crackd the No Egg Egg* and *Ogg* have good reviews. Both can also be used in baking as egg substitutes, too. In baking, there are so many choices to replace eggs using everyday ingredients (apple sauce, mashed banana, ground flax seed or chia seed, Silken tofu, arrowroot powder, etc.). In Australia, there's also Orgran Vegan Easy Egg. There is a burgeoning vegan product market. I wouldn't be surprised if there were more commercial egg replacements and other animal product replacements out there by the time you pick up this book!

You Scream, We Scream, We All Scream for Vegan Ice Cream

Ice Cream that baby cows and their mothers didn't have to scream for. Where do I start? There are almost too many for my spreading waistline! Vegan Ice Creams, *Soy Delicious*, *Tofutti Cuties*, all of the major ice cream lines have added vegan versions. I like *Tofutti* sour cream, Kite Hill vanilla yogurt, raspberries, *Soy Delicious* chocolate frozen dessert, and non-dairy cream whip (coconut whip cream is also amazing), all in a glass! Superb!

Whether it's coffee creamer, cream cheese, whipped cream, ice cream or yoghurt you are looking for, there is no longer any need to choose dairy versions. Today, any good health food store or large grocery food chain will be able to provide you with vegan, cruelty-free alternatives for all of these products.

ADOPT THE FOUR FOOD GROUPS

Would you believe that two thirds of American adults and one third of American children are overweight or obese?

The Physicians Committee for Responsible Medicine is an independent group of over 16,000 doctors, also known as PCRM. Their messages are independent and free from any financial support by the pharmaceutical industry or other industries that may have a vested interest in your consumer dollar. PCRM doctors recommend the nutrient-rich four main daily food groups: fruit, vegetables, grain and legumes. (Legumes is a fancy word for beans, peas and lentils, etc.)

These food groups are dense in fiber, calcium, nutrients and minerals – and they are versatile. They are easy to use creatively in recipes and are naturally delicious! Think hummus, falafel, dahl, chili, split pea soup. The list goes on and on.

Check out **PCRM.org** for more free resources.

EDUCATE YOURSELF

Research for yourself why consuming animal-based products is cruel, environmentally destructive and unhealthy for people.

Vegancalculator.com tabulates how many animals, trees and how much fresh water and oxygen you save each day by going vegan.

In 1980, I read an article about an undercover investigation at a slaughterhouse in the *Toronto Sun* newspaper. When I saw the photos of the pigs who were so obviously suffering, I cried while reading the news article. It changed my life. Today, many people are educated by documentaries such as *Earthlings, The Heart Whisperer* both by filmmaker Shaun Monson, *What the Health, Cowspiracy, The Game Changers*, or news reports about undercover cruelty investigations. They may see a shorter video on Facebook or YouTube that will open the mind to questions or even a *Be an Animal Hero* or *Animal Hero Kids* video.

*Check out the **Animal Hero Crew plant milk taste tests and recipe videos** on the Vegan Videos page of BEanANIMALHERO.org.

Vegolution Solutions:
Vegan Lives Advice

"Bring it on down to Veganville."

—Justin Timberlake

I f you haven't already seen the *Saturday Night Live* skit with Justin Timberlake, Google it now. It's great fun. After all, vegans just want to have fun and not hurt anyone in the process. Here are some surefire ways to help those curious friends and family "Bring it on down to Veganville."

1. Throw a lot of dinner parties, picnics, barbecues preferably with great music in a nice setting. Invite friends, family and neighbors over and wow them with your delicious vegan cooking.

2. Go grocery shopping with your friends and family so that they see what you buy at the grocery store. Introduce them to the vegan food items at your local grocery or health food store and encourage them to try several new products they might like. Don't be shy about opening your fridge when visitors are over and offer taste samples. Give away vegan foods/products that they like to get them hooked! I personally have given away bags of vegan marshmallows, packets of vegan cheese, and packages of smoked apple and sage vegan sausages. If they have them, they will eat them. Then, if they really liked the product, they are likely to go out and buy it again.

3. Cook with your friends, family, and maybe even neighbors so they see what you prepare, how you prepare it, and that it is not too hard to make but definitely delicious.

4. Talk food with your friends, family and neighbors but not in a preachy way. Talk about a new restaurant you tried, a new recipe you loved, what produce is in season, the new vegan ice cream that was just released. Be a vegan foodie!

5. Always send vegan alternatives when your kids go to birthday parties, school parties, sleepovers: vegan pizza, coconut ice cream, healthier vegan snacks like organic corn chips and guacamole. If you can afford it, send enough for everyone to try. Sometimes, local vegan restaurants will help with giving their food out at local events and may give you good deals in exchange for giving out their flyers to get new customers.

6. Let your kids' teachers know that your family is vegan by asking if you can bring in vegan treats. Schools are hesitant to take food someone has made at home, so closed containers are normally what is requested. Maybe your kids can bring in food to share for a class project or presentation. They can do a project on veganism or a sort of show-and-tell on being vegan and include some information about the student's favorite singers, actors or athletes who are vegan.

7. Host holiday meals at your house and see if you can get live music or something to make it really special. This way, family members will have a delicious family feast, and not even think about the fact that they are eating all vegan. Who needs a dead bird when you can have a roast Tofurky with **Roasted Veggies and The Best Gravy in the World** (see recipe on page 110)!

8. Give gift certificates for local vegan restaurants and health food stores, vegan cookbooks, books about vegan health, a copy of *Animal Hero Kids – Voices for the Voiceless, Veganza Animal Heroes Series* books and other animal liberation books. Thank restaurants you visit for having vegan options and encourage stores, bakeries and restaurants to offer more vegan options.

Top **7** Answers to FAQ

"We must stand together and speak up to save our planet, not just for us, but for our future generations. I have been vegan now for eight years, I just can't go on in my life knowing what's going on and not doing anything about it."

—Billie Eilish

You will get all kinds of questions, some genuinely curious, some an attempt to tease or dismiss the credence of being vegan. It's amazing how many of your friends and family become "concerned" about your nutritional intake, world hunger, and the life and feelings of plants when you go vegan.

One reminder Monique Martinez, the wonderful artist of Veganza, gives is to remember that we were not all vegan at birth. We had to realize why it is important to go vegan, some in a series of steps. So, try not to judge or be on your high horse. Okay, don't ride horses at all. One friend simply states that he is cruelty-free when the subject of being vegan comes up.

I went vegetarian in 1980 and vegan in 1985 or 1986 (I truly don't recall what year. I was so busy organizing, protesting and investigating.) If I had a dollar for every time I have been asked these questions, I would be able to open the *Be an Animal Hero* dream education center and amusement park that I have envisioned for so long!

The good news is that your answers often lead to people considering their choices, and you won't even know it at the time. There are multiple answers for each question. Your choice of answer may depend on the situation and on the person you are speaking with.

1. Where do you get your protein?

The animals whose flesh people are eating all got their protein from plants. You now go directly to the source of the protein, without the animal fat, animal cruelty and climate destruction.

We are taught to believe protein can only come from eating animals. 42 percent of the calories in broccoli are pure protein without the animal fats, animal cruelty and damage to the Earth and that's just one example of the beans, veggies, veggie burgers, etc. They are all in forms of usable, 'good for you' protein.

2. What about the starving children?

World hunger can be solved by eating vegetable-based foods directly. It takes 16 pounds of grain to produce one pound of 'meat'. We can feed more people on a vegan diet than on an omnivorous diet. One acre of land can produce 27,000 pounds of potatoes or 150 pounds of cow flesh. World resources are better spent on feeding more people plant-based foods, using fewer resources (soil, water, etc.).

3. What about plants? Don't they have feelings too?

Plants do not have a central nervous system and don't bleed and feel pain in the same way you or your dog would.
If you were driving on the road and there was a pig or a plant, (you can alternate with a raccoon or broccoli, a dog with a carrot... you get the idea), which would you swerve to avoid hitting?
If you truly care about the lives of plants, then eating plants directly rather than multiplied through the flesh of the animals saves more plants. It takes 14–16 pounds of grain to produce one pound of 'meat'.

4. We are at the top of the food chain, aren't we? So, aren't humans supposed to eat meat? That's why we have incisors.

The silverback mountain gorilla's incisors can measure two inches in length. They are a close relative to humans, and yet they eat mainly plants.

The intestinal length of true carnivores is shorter in order to be able to completely digest food in 2–4 hours. The intestinal track of lions is three times the length of their body, measured from head to tail.

A human intestinal track is approximately 9 times the length of the human body, measured the same way you would a lion, not counting the legs of the human. Herbivores digest their food in 12–24 hours.

The intestinal length is important, so the flesh doesn't rot on the way out. Plus, strong digestive acids in the saliva and stomach of a true carnivore break down any rotting flesh quicker. This means that they are less affected by E. coli and salmonella. The World Health Organization (WHO) states that 230,000 people a year die from foodborne illnesses caused by E. coli and salmonella bacteria.

If we were natural carnivores, we would just leap on an animal and tear it apart with our teeth and eat it raw. A good example is if a child had a choice of playing with or eating a piglet or a strawberry. Which would they eat, and which would they play with or pat?

5. If we stopped eating animals, wouldn't we be overrun with animals?

No, we would not be moving cows, pigs or chickens out of the driveway before going to work. It's a natural evolution of supply and demand. Currently, animals are artificially inseminated to kill to sell for people to eat. If the demand to eat flesh is reduced, then there's no point in artificially inseminating, feeding and housing 'farm' animals to have the result of not making money. That's why so many farmers are deciding to go into the plant-based food system instead. Elmhurst Dairy, an iconic cow's milk company since 1925 now offers hazelnut, oat, and walnut plant milks instead. They even sell plant-based milk lattes. This is how economies adapt to progress. However, when our tax dollars go to artificially subsidize outdated, planet damaging, cruel products, then we do have a problem.

6. Vegans are weak and skinny. There's no way you can build real muscle as a vegan, is there?

When I go into group homes and speak to teens, especially males, I always bring facts about vegan bodybuilders who are built! Sometimes, I am even fortunate enough to have Korin Sutton, a professional vegan bodybuilder, join me. One of the examples he gives in his presentation is the strongest primate in the world, the silverback mountain gorilla. Korin is a walking advertisement for strong, muscular vegans. There are so many in Florida! Torre Washington, Korin Sutton, Julian Gibson-Serrette, Yvonne Gibson-Serrette, and Geoff Palmer just to name a few. The movie *Game Changers* knocks the belief in vegans not building muscle out of the water. Four-time Guinness World Records record breaker strongman Patrick Baboumian is also a vegan.

7. If you were trapped on a deserted island, would you kill and eat an animal to survive?

What if you were not trapped on a deserted island and you had access to a bounty of delicious food where you did not have to kill anyone? This scenario is a reality. We do have so many healthier, scrumptious choices where no animals have to be harmed. Why eat animals if we do not need to from a nutritional perspective and not eating animals means not keeping them captive, keeping them from their young in an unnatural life, often in inhumane conditions. Not eating animals means not making animals suffer and not killing animals.

If ever you are trapped on a deserted island, you can figure out what you need to do to survive but, in the meantime, why not try going vegan for a while and see how it feels? The animals, the Earth and your health will thank you.

Veganza Animal Heroes Series – Liberation

Book Club
Discussion Questions

1. Who are the two main reporter characters in this book?

2. What symbolic importance does the name Phoenix hold for the main human character?

3. What parts of the story are inspired by Celtic mythological folklore?

4. Why does the animal world need hero rescuers?

5. How many rescues take place in the story and what type of rescues?

6. What are the three main animal heroes' magic powers?

7. Can you think of a new animal hero character to feature in the next book?

8. What is the point of the author's subtitles peppered throughout the book?

9. Who would you like to see rescued, any species, including human, and included in the next *Veganza Animal Heroes* book?

10. What animal injustice issue could be tackled in the next *Veganza Animal Heroes* book?

Works Cited

Pages 119–124 Veganza's Vegan Tips: Replacing Animal Products—Three Easy Steps to Go Vegan:
Forbes, June 9, 2021, article title "The Opportunities for Plant Based Dairy Alternatives"
Fact: 48 percent of consumers purchased plant milks in the U.S in 2019.

Page 41 Lolita liberation story:
Scientific American. May 21, 2018, article title "Free Lolita the Killer Whale"
Fact: Lolita's mother is still alive in her resident pod.
Note: **TheVegancalculator.com** has proved a valuable resource.

Pages 113–115 Why Vegan?—Vegan for the Animals
Fact: The numbers of land animals and fish killed
BiteSizedVegan.org and AnimalClock.org

ACKNOWLEDGEMENTS

Lovey is my constant comforting companion, a steady, non-judgmental love. She is 22 years old at the time of writing this in 2022. When I write, she is always beside me, her paw touching my side. When I visit schools to do humane education programs, she knows she will always be safe as long as I hold her. The collective "awe" heard in school assemblies when students see her partially crippled, seal like walk toddle across the stage embodies the audiences' high regard for her well-being.

I met Tanjah Karvonen during my Toronto animal activism over thirty-two years ago. Her editorial organizational skills and strength of planning is nothing short of miraculous. I am so fortunate to benefit from her steady, patient voice of reason pointing out the necessary formats to be adhered to. I appreciate her kindness and attention to detail and genuine friendship.

To an Anonymous donor (you know who you are, I don't) who believes in heartwarming stories to inspire the mainstream to make vegan choices, thank you for your trust and your vote of confidence.

To my wife, Rebecca Hewitt, who keeps the house going when she is the writer or activist "widow". Thanks for your support and belief in my ability to make a dent in the giant corporate wall of animal suffering.

My mum, Irene Tyrrell, like so many mums, provides encouragement using undiplomatic terms. She's the only one who will tell you when you're gaining weight or completely overdoing it, a vital honest role I am fortunate to benefit from. Thank you, Mum, for being in my corner.

The extraordinary illustrative art of Monique Martinez gives life to Veganza's rich world of defense, rescue and magic.

Ron Nistico Palamara is my dear friend whose support and belief in the mission of rescuing animals is boundless. Ron believes in the potential for positive change through the stories I tell. His continued confidence in my skill to empower others to compassionate action is priceless.

Thank you to Erin Fontes for her humor, her can-do attitude and sense of order. She balances achieving our goals with the non-profit charity DBA *Be an Animal Hero*, a project of animalherokids.org with friendship and fun, too.

Thanks to Dad for always being at the end of the phone with advice and for saving me from the motorcycle gang when I was 16 (a true story for another book). Thanks Dad and Pauline for the frothy soy coffees and long chats over scrumptious vegan breakfasts.

Thank you to my supportive manuscript readers for the set of fresh eyes after I go "word blind" like Patti Roth, who can be trusted to rise to the occasion.

I so appreciate the reporter expertise filter of Alexi Wyatt for my writing for grants and news releases. I am fortunate to benefit from Alexi's friendship. Sean Russell is also a trusted positive ally.

Thank you to Maggie Baird, the founder of Support and Feed and mother to Billie Eilish and Finneas O'Connell, for her help empowering youth by being a guest on the videos we produce. Maggie and Billie make cameo appearances in the book.

My Irish cousins, the Tyrrell family, are a wealth of knowledge. The Tyrrells, including Niall Tyrrell and his husband Oliver McCabe and Helen Tyrrell, too, are a generous crew whose help was invaluable in forming the Wicklow segment of the story.

In Ireland, I was thrilled to meet some of the Happy Pear tribe: Dave, Steve and Darragh Flynn and Sara Fawsitt. The Happy Pear tribe are like an Irish vegan mecca. I met them on a visit to Greystones, Wicklow, Ireland. They are such a positive fun group. The twins swim in the sea in the morning and offer a breakfast of porridge after to any swimmers who wish to join them.

Sherry Schlueter and Shelly Schlueter are two sisters who are each strong animal advocates in their own right. I appreciate their emotional, positive support more than they know.

I appreciate Ingrid Newkirk, founder of PETA, for always being there to give advice and for being so supportive of my mission to help other animals since 1983.

ABOUT THE AUTHOR

Susan Hargreaves is a *Skipping Stones Honor* award-winning author, a kindness educator, a long time vegan, speaker and activist. She has rehabilitated wildlife and investigated animal cruelty in circuses, rodeos, aquariums and in the animal-based agriculture industry. Susan became active in the animal rights movement in 1980. She hosted and piloted the first animal rights radio series in both Canada and in the United States. Her relentless and lengthy journey to aid animals is the subject of an original short documentary by the renowned *Earthlings* director, Shaun Monson, entitled *The Heart Whisperer*.

Susan created the first interactive dramatizations in schools to create an understanding of the plight of other animals. She founded the youth-empowering charity *Animal Hero Kids* and created the *Be an Animal Hero* project to prevent animal cruelty she witnessed from an early age, by fostering empathy leading to informed, compassionate choices. Susan continues to collaborate with national and international organizations and is a regular speaker at the largest animal rights conference in the world: Animal Rights National Conference. Susan is a grassroots and global organizer at the frontlines of animal rights advocacy and protection. Her previous books are *Animal Hero Kids—Voices for the Voiceless,* Volume 1 and 2, and the *Veganza Animal Hero* picture book.

Susan Hargreaves has been featured, extensively, on national and international news stories speaking out for other animals to live unharmed.

She is the recipient of the Compassionate Educator Award by Archbishop R. McKenzie, the Eco-Hero Humane and Environmental Education Award, the Distinguished Educator Award presented by Share the World-Teachkind, the Wings Award for Advancing Unique Partnerships by the Pegasus Foundation and the Shining World Leadership Award by the Supreme Master Ching Hai International Association. Susan was heralded in the *Best Environmentalists List* by the *Broward Palm Beach New Times*.

Susan earned emigration into the United States in the person of extraordinary ability category – reserved for Olympic athletes – for her groundbreaking humane education programs. The U.S. government ascertained she is in the top 5 percent of her field.

Susan can be booked to speak, virtually or in person, at your library, bookstore, school or club, and is available for news interviews and to comment on current animal issues. She can be contacted at SusanHargreaves.com or BEanANIMALHERO.org.

Susan says, "Lovey and I thrive on interactive, lively discussions about how we can all be animal heroes by changing our choices."

The Heart Whisperer film by *Earthlings* creator, Shaun Monson, tells the story of one woman's relentless pursuit to push the boundaries of our compassion and includes never before seen footage of direct activism. This film is ideal for college or university classes on the subject of ethics, evolving societies, the effect of documentary journalism or the politics of change. You can book Susan to speak at colleges or universities and screen this film with a complimentary vegan food sampling.

Vegan farmed animal sanctuaries are welcome to join the developing global partnerships program of the *Be an Animal Hero* project. Find out more about this collaborative campaign by going to the education page of BEanANIMALHERO.org.

Made in the USA
Columbia, SC
06 September 2023

cd2e4fbb-402a-4c00-8848-74146ffef7eeR01